Pretty
Face

Also by Mary Hogan

THE SERIOUS KISS

PERFECT GIRL

Pretty Face

Mary Hogan

HARPER TEEN

An Imprint of HarperCollins*Publishers*

HarperTeen is an imprint of HarperCollins Publishers.

Pretty Face

Library of Congress Cataloging-in-Publication Data
Hogan, Mary, 1957–
  Pretty face / by Mary Hogan. — 1st ed.
    p. cm.
  Summary: When an overweight high school student from Santa Monica spends the summer in Italy, she learns to relish life and understand the true meaning of beauty.
  ISBN 978-0-06-084111-9 (trade bdg.)
  ISBN 978-0-06-084112-6 (lib. bdg.)
  [1. Self-acceptance—Fiction. 2. Weight control—Fiction. 3. Dating (Social customs)—Fiction. 4. Italy—Fiction. 5. Santa Monica (Calif.)—Fiction.] I. Title.
PZ7.H683125Pr 2008   2007011869
[Fic]—dc22   CIP
                                                                      AC

Typography by Sasha Illingworth
1 2 3 4 5 6 7 8 9 10
❖
First Edition

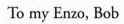

To my Enzo, Bob

Acknowledgments

Mille grazie to my amazing editor, Amanda Maciel, who has never made a suggestion that I didn't like and think, "Of course!" A million thanks, also, to Laura Langlie for always giving me the right advice and guidance. And, enormous *gratitudine* to the people of beautiful Assisi, Italy, for their warm welcome and great (!) food. I can't wait to come back.

One

Mom bought me a digital scale.

"So you can't lie to yourself," she said. I glared at her, my right foot jutting forward.

"God, Mom," I scoffed. "I mean, *God.*"

What else could I say? She was totally right. Yesterday, I shunted my rusty old IKEA scale all over the bathroom floor looking for the most favorable reading. Turns out, you can shave a full five pounds off if you put the bottom half of the scale on the bath mat, hang your toes off the front, and squint.

Today, it's no such luck. The digital scale won't read anything at all unless it's on a level surface. Thanks a lot, Mom.

Behind the locked bathroom door, I pee, kick off my

slippers, drop my robe, step out of my pajama pants, and lift my cotton cami over my head. Taking a deep breath, I exhale hard, blowing all the air out of my body. Contracting it as much as possible. Then I step on my new digital scale.

I hear a sound.

Beep. Then a loud, robotic voice.

"One hundred and—"

Horrified, I leap off the scale. Mom bought me a scale that talks!? Is she out of her mind? Not only do I have to see the bloated number glow accusingly at me in a hideous green light, I have to *hear* the bad news, too? What else will it say?

Shave your legs, slacker. Would a pedicure kill you? Think you'll ever have a boyfriend with those thighs?

Mom shrieks through the closed bathroom door. "I'm calling Dr. Weinstein."

"Mother!" I shriek back. "Can't I have any privacy?"

"Your brother weighs less than you, Hayley. Do you want to weigh more than a boy?"

"His brain is only an ounce. Mine is packed with weighty knowledge."

Mom presses her mouth up to the doorjamb. "I'm only thinking of your health."

I roll my eyes and turn on the shower.

"If you keep going like this," she says into the crack of the door, "you're going to weigh as much as two people."

"I've always wanted a sister," I reply. Then I get in the

shower and let the hot water drown out my mother's voice.

The awful scale accusation echoes through my brain. Thirty pounds from where I should be. If only I were taller— five foot eleven, instead of five foot five! I press my eyes shut, feel the disgusting curve of my bowling-ball belly as I soap up. My arms are soft and fleshy. Even my toes are fat.

I hate myself.

Turning the cold water down, I feel my skin burn. I stand there as long as I can take it.

"Today," I say out loud, "I will be *good*. Salad for lunch. No dressing."

Quickly washing and rinsing my long brown hair, I step out of the shower and grab a towel before I can see my hideous pink reflection in the steamy bathroom mirror.

"Yes," I repeat. "Today I'll be good."

Mom is gone. Ragging on Dad somewhere, no doubt. Which is good because no way can I stomach one of her evangelical lectures about portion control. There's nothing worse than a former fatty who found God in fresh fruits and vegetables.

"If I can do it, you can, too!" she chirps constantly.

"Can you find the square root of sixty-four?" I asked her.

"Hayley . . . ," she said, with a disapproving look.

"See?" I replied. "We can't both do everything. There *are* differences between the two of us."

Mom doesn't get it. I *want* to be thin. Hell, I want to be America's Next Top Model, if only to out-bitch the other anorexics. But something goes awry every time I try. I don't know what it is. I think I'm improperly wired. My need to feed is stronger than my desire to—literally—fit in.

Standing before my open closet door, I flip through my clothes. Then I moan. They can put a lunar rover on Mars! Why can't they make jeans that don't make my ass look like Jupiter?

Two

It's a sunny day. Of course. It's always a sunny day in Southern California. And this morning, even the sidewalks are glowing bright yellow. Jackie waits for me in front of her house, eating a granola bar.

"Here," she says, hopping in my car. "I brought one for you."

"I already had breakfast," I lie.

"Whatever."

Jackie opens the glove compartment of my old Saturn and tosses the granola bar inside. She props her feet on my dash as I drive us to school.

"You know Randy? That idiot in my Graphic Design class?"

5

I nod.

"He e-mailed me this Photoshop collage of a woman made from the different body parts of supermodels."

"How inventive," I say dryly.

"It was like Gisele's right boob, Naomi's left leg, Kate's belly button—"

"I get the picture."

We turn left on La Mesa Drive, another left on Ocean.

"The freaky thing is, she looks awesome."

"Who?" I ask. "Gisele? Naomi?"

Jackie groans. "Are you listening, Hayley?"

"Of course I'm listening," I say.

Truth is, I'm not. Not fully. Jackie chatters like this every day. She's one of those "morning people." I'm not sure what time of day I am. Probably midnight, when it's dark and so silent even scales don't talk.

"You were saying?"

Jackie and I have been best friends since Ms. Rafter paired us up for the rope climb in sixth-grade gym class. Neither one of us got very high. I was mortified, convinced from the start that my flaccid arms could never hoist my heft up a skinny little rope. Jackie was more philosophical about it.

"I'm going to be a fashion designer," she said. "If this were a rope *necklace*, I'd be interested."

She half-heartedly pulled herself up a few feet, while I huffed and puffed and turned red in the face.

Finally giving up, I said, "Maybe I'll be a fashion designer, too."

We laughed. I liked her instantly, even though she's thin and can eat like a truck driver. At least she's not blond. We're both brunettes. Though, admittedly, Jackie has a blond personality. Me, let's just say I'm woefully short on highlights of any kind. Jackie walks through life as if every moment is her first. She takes on new situations with an open face and an open heart. She even dismantled the caller ID on her cell because, she said, "Why ruin the surprise?"

I want to know what's about to hit me. I brace myself for life even as I watch my best friend *em*brace it. Like last week when I drummed up the nerve to ask Drew Wyler if he wanted to hang out with me at the Promenade this weekend. He said, "Sure. Will Jackie be there?"

"You want her to be?" I asked him.

"Why not?"

Dazed, I spent the whole week dissecting our conversation. Did he want to go *out* with my BFF? Or, is it just more fun when she's around? Was he asking to be polite, because Jackie and I are *always* shopping on the Promenade together?

"Drew is cool," Jackie said innocently, when I suggested our threesome. "But, I thought you liked him. Why do you want me there?"

What could I say? *I don't. Drew does. Or does he?*

Feigning indifference, I didn't respond. Jackie shrugged and forgot about it. I obsessed for days.

Why is everything so damn hard?

"The point is," Jackie says in the car, "a model's body

parts are interchangeable. However you mix them up, they are going to look hot. Even though Randy is a jerk, I think he makes an interesting social statement. Don't you?"

"Models are perfect! Call the six-o'clock news!"

As Jackie playfully gives me the finger, I notice that even her middle digit is much thinner than mine.

"Do we have time for a Starbucks?" she asks.

I check my watch. "If there's no line."

With a final left onto Wilshire Boulevard, I pull into the Starbucks parking lot, three doors away from school. Jackie hops out.

"Strawberry Frap?" she asks.

I sigh. A venti Strawberries and Crème Frappuccino with whipped cream is seven hundred and fifty calories. I looked it up. Even though my stomach is growling, I'm going to be good today. My goal: to have my new bathroom scale whisper praise in my ear.

I can barely feel you. Who needs shaved legs when they look this good in pants?

"Well?" Jackie asks.

"Okay," I say, pulling money out of my backpack. "But only a grande. And no whipped cream."

Jackie skips off into the store. The moment she's out of sight, I reach into the glove box and devour the granola bar before I even know what I'm doing.

Three

Pacific High is five blocks from the beach. Our apartment is about half a mile away, and Jackie's house is a bit beyond that. We could walk to school, but this is Los Angeles—Santa Monica, to be exact—and the only people who walk are the homeless and cleaning ladies.

The school bell rings just as I'm feeling the last cool swallow of Frap slither down my throat.

"Baja Fresh for lunch?" Jackie yells as she dashes to class. "It's meatball grinder day in the cafeteria."

"Yeah, okay," I call after her. They have salads at Baja Fresh, right?

Smoothing my straight hair down my neck, checking my teeth for gloss smudge, and making sure my pockets are flat on my too-tight jeans, I walk into first period.

"Hey," he says as I curl into the desk next to his.

"Hey," I repeat, sucking my stomach in.

His sandy hair isn't even combed and he's still gorgeous.

Drew Wyler and I are in Advanced Placement English together. Which is why my brain is so weighted down in the morning. Love is heavy. So is literature. When they're not cramming Shakespeare down our throats, it's Homer. (Not Simpson, unfortunately.) And I don't care how good Nicole Kidman was in that movie about Virginia Woolf; *Mrs. Dalloway* is unreadable. I did like *The Great Gatsby*, though, which I read over the summer. Why can't more of the classics be about hunky rich guys who fall for other men's wives?

I fell for Drew on the first day of class.

"Is this the first level of Dante's *Inferno*?" he asked me, pointing to the semester's reading list.

I smiled stiffly, too stunned by his literary reference to reply. Had he already read Dante? Though it's my third year in high school, it's my first year in AP English. Was I already hopelessly behind?

Drew's black eyes peered out through John Lennon glasses. His wavy hair fell over his forehead and curled around his ears. The hollows of his cheeks indented like perfect inverted parentheses.

Clearly, Drew Wyler was way out of my league.

Still, how can you tell your heart not to take a swing?

"Did you see this honking syllabus?" another student asked me.

I nodded. But I was lying. I only had eyes for Drew.

I'd seen Drew Wyler around campus all last year, and a few times at the pier. Girls were around him a lot, but he never hooked up with anyone in particular. And it was a badly kept secret that he didn't live in Santa Monica. His uncle had an apartment on Marguerita Avenue, which he used as the address that got him into Pacific High. I heard he lived in Inglewood, a freeway drive away. But, he'd never say for sure, 'cause if the principal found out, he'd be booted out of here.

"Um, what time you wanna meet on Saturday?" I ask him quietly.

"Saturday?"

My heart sinks. He's forgotten already?

"The Promenade?" I say. "Hanging out?"

"Oh, yeah."

He reaches down to the floor and pulls his notebook out of his pack. My Strawberry Frap sits cold in my gut.

"I can get us into any movie for free," I say, leaning across the aisle between us, trying not to sound as desperate as I feel. "I work at the Cineplex part-time."

"Hayley?"

Ms. Antonucci, our teacher, looks at me with her eyebrows raised.

"Are we interrupting your social intercourse?" she asks.

"No," I say. "I believe in social abstinence before marriage."

The class laughs. Ms. Antonucci laughs, too. But the only sound that matters is Drew's chuckle beside me. When he smiles, his whole face changes. Like Ewan McGregor's. You can't help but smile back when you see it.

"Saturday at ten," he whispers.

four

"If I wash these jeans tonight, I'll have to wear them tomorrow so they won't be too tight on Saturday. That's three days in a row. Do you think anyone will notice?"

"What about that cute skirt you bought?" Jackie asks. Then she orders a pork carnita from the hottie in the Baja Fresh shirt.

Jackie's answer to my question lets me know what I already know. *Everyone* will notice. This is Santa Monica. Los Angeles, California. Narcissus unable to turn away from his own reflection. Here, every waiter is an actor, and every actress is twenty pounds underweight because the camera adds fifteen. This is the city next to the Venice Beach boardwalk and Malibu, where women shop in bikini tops and "shave" their legs with lasers. On a quiet afternoon, you can almost hear the sound of fat being sucked through liposuction cannulas. Three girls in my school had boob jobs over spring break.

"I'll have the Baja salad," I say to the guy at the register. "With chicken."

He hands us a vibrating pager, and we find a table near the window.

"That skirt looks too needy," I tell Jackie. "I want to seem casual. Like I don't care."

"Wear it with a double cami and flip-flops. You'll look casual *and* cool."

I shoot Jackie a look. "A cami? Sleeveless in front of the boy I want to see naked? Get real."

"Your arms are fine, Hayley. And you have *such* a pretty face."

There it is. The kiss of death. She might as well have told me I have a great personality.

"Hello, chickies."

Lindsay Whittaker sashays past our table on her way to the salsa bar. Her entourage—Chloe, Bethany, Lacey, and some other "E" whose name I can never remember—smiles at us in that fake way that makes me want to trip them. In fact, I poke my toe out slightly. But not enough to look like it's on purpose.

"You're looking very . . . perky," I say to Lacey, one (two?) of the spring break boob jobs.

"Waiting for nachos, Hayley?" she shoots back. "With extra cheese?"

"Hey, Bethany," Jackie pipes up. "How'd you do on that Spanish quiz?"

"*Bueno.*"

"*Yo, tambien,*" Jackie says, giggling. The "E's" giggle, too.

Jackie is cliqueless. She gets along with everybody. I'm cliqueless, too. I get along with her. I do see irony in the fact that Jackie and I are both technical "E's" since our names end in that sound, but I'd never be invited into Lindsay's crew. Not that I'd want to be. They're totally superficial. Last Christmas, they all got gift certificates for Brite Smile treatments. I asked for a gift certificate to Amazon, but Mom bought me an exercise bike instead.

Bzzzzzz.

The pager lights up and vibrates. I don't move. No way am I getting up in front of the "E's" and giving them a full-on view of my rear.

"I'll get our food," Jackie says, hopping up.

Thank God I got a salad.

Lindsay and the other girls help themselves to the free salsa bar. It's their lunch. Topped with a sprinkling of cilantro. They wouldn't be caught dead eating a carb. You'd think management would kick them out, but when the "E's" arrive, the "B's" are never far behind. Drooling boys who order burritos and quesadillas and extra-large sides of chips with guac. God, I hope Drew Wyler isn't one of them.

five

Turns out, Drew is a brown-bagger. You'd think I would have known that with the gazillion hours I'd spent trying to appear like I'm not looking for him all over campus.

Today, Friday, I decide to pull some private-eye action and follow him at lunch. Before I make a complete fool of myself at the Promenade tomorrow, I need to make sure he's not meeting some skank from Inglewood.

I won't let Jackie come with me.

"You'll blow my cover," I say.

It's a total lie. Truth is, if Drew spots us following him, I don't want his eyes to light up when he sees Jackie. The only time I want him seeing her is when she's covered with guys that could kick his ass. Which is often. Jackie is friends with several guys on the football team, because her older brother, Ty, is a star somethingback. He's not a *quarter*back, that much I know. But he catches the football a lot and runs zigzag across the field and dances in the end zone. When I'm with him, I notice that everyone else wants to be with him, too. Like it is with Jackie. It must be something in their DNA.

"Take these." Jackie hands me her oversize sunglasses. "Drew may recognize you in yours."

I feel like a giant fly in her glasses, but she has a point. Drew *has* seen me in my knock-off aviators.

"Buena suerte," she says.

"Thanks. I think." I take Latin. Don't ask.

Suddenly, there he is.

Wearing jeans rolled at the cuff, brown Pumas, and a white T-shirt, Drew leaves campus for Ocean Avenue. Bug Eye—me—in hot pursuit. Instantly, I realize what "hot" pursuit means. My armpits get damp right away. And my head sweats. Who has a sweaty scalp?

Drew walks *fast*. He doesn't seem to be rushing, but his long legs carry him far ahead of me. It's a sunny day (of course). Rays flicker off the Pacific Ocean like butterflies. As I scurry along, I feel the intermittent cool shade of palm trees. I wish I hadn't worn high-heeled clogs. My bare feet are sliding all over inside them. My toes keep smashing to the front. But heels elongate my legs. Even though clogs condense my toes.

At Colorado Avenue, Drew takes a right onto the Santa Monica pier. He walks under the arch, past the carousel. By the time I get close, he's seated on a bench, gazing out at the ocean. Alone.

If I wasn't so out of breath, I'd heave a sigh of relief. As it is, I just heave.

"Hayley?"

For some reason known only to parapsychologists, Drew senses my existence and turns around. Or, did he recognize my heavy breathing . . . ?

"Oh, hi, Drew," I say casually. "Fan—"

I almost say, "Fancy meeting you here." Like a complete and total wack job. Like we're in a Jane Austen novel or something. Blushing intensely, I notice I'm now panting.

"Want to sit down?" Drew asks.

"Do I look like I need to?" I snap. Then, I shut my eyes and quietly ask God why I was ever born.

Drew laughs. "A little," he says.

My clogs sound like horse hooves as I clomp across the wooden pier to Drew's bench. I try to channel Calista Flockhart and sit softly, but the bench definitely gives a bit under the weight of my very *un*-Calista-like ass.

"Where's your lunch?" Drew asks.

"I ate already," I lie.

Nodding, Drew opens his brown bag and takes out a peanut butter sandwich.

"Want half?" he asks.

"No, thanks."

He nods again and takes a bite. The two of us sit there—Drew chewing and watching the waves, me trying not to stare at his amazing jaw—until I finally think of the perfect thing to say.

"What a sunny day!"

Six

I am *such* an ass! I am the assiest of all asses. I bray in my sleep. The weather? I'm sitting next to a boy who actually *reads* Dante, and I talk about the *sun* in Southern California?

Drew doesn't answer. He's too cool to waste time with meaningless small talk. He just nods, chews his sandwich, and takes a swig of Snapple. If I could move, I'd clomp my squishy, toe-crushing clogs over to the railing and heave my fat, assiest ass over.

"You read *Trailers* yet?" he asks, breaking the screaming silence.

"Trailers? Like movie trailers?"

"No. It's a graphic novel about this kid who has to bury

the body after his mom offs somebody."

"Oh," I say, grossed out. But at least it sounds more interesting than the *Iliad*. Though, that Trojan Horse idea was inspired.

"Would you ever do that?" Drew asks me. "Cover for your mother like that? Bury a dead body?"

I think for a moment. The only person I can imagine my mother killing is my dad. And it would be some sort of slow poisoning with tofu. Which, in a way, we're enduring right now. An excruciating, nightly torture.

"A cup of tofu has sixteen grams of protein!" Mom said last night.

"And a cheeseburger has thirty," I replied. One of the few things I remembered from Health class. That, and the fact that a bulky female condom exists, though I can't imagine anyone ever wearing it.

"No," I say to Drew. "I don't think I'd bury a dead body."

"You'd turn your own mother in?"

"Can't I just do nothing? Pretend I don't know?"

"You could," he says, "but the knowledge would eat away at you until you were nothing but an empty shell of a person."

Before considering how unsexy it is, I pat my plump thighs and say, "I could live with that."

Drew laughs. My whole body melts into the warm, wooden bench. He wouldn't invite me to sit down if he didn't like me, would he? He wouldn't laugh if he thought I was a loser . . . would he?

Suddenly, it's all perfectly clear. What I need to do is crank it up a notch. Be seductive. Stop cracking jokes and start flirting. Let Drew know I'm available. I got an A in that Health class. I know what goes on between the sheets. It's time to put my knowledge into action.

Right now, however, I'm frozen. Sadly, I can't summon sexuality on demand. Not when I'm sweating and probably getting sunstroke.

Tomorrow, at the Promenade, I'll be ready. Saturday is the day I make my move.

Seven

"Honestly," Mom says at dinner, "tofu is completely misunderstood."

Collectively, my younger brother, Quinn, my dad, and I groan. The kitchen smells like dirty socks. We all have glum faces around the table.

"It's really just a sponge for other flavors," she continues. "Like tonight's kale casserole. The tofu in it has soaked up the vegetarian broth."

Thank God Jackie and I stopped by Mickey D's on the way home from school to share a large fries.

Dad asks, "Why can't it soak up the juice from a porterhouse steak?"

"John," Mom says, with an elaborate sigh. "You want

another heart attack? Is that what you want?"

My father sighs elaborately too.

Technically, Dad *didn't* have a heart attack last summer when he collapsed while installing new carbon monoxide detectors in our building. The ER docs called it a "cardiac event."

"Event?" Mom had shrieked, wild-eyed. "The Academy Awards is an *event*. I found my husband facedown in the hallway of our apartment building!"

"He fainted as a result of a heart arrhythmia, which was exacerbated by an arterial blockage," the doctor explained patiently.

"What?!" Mom shrieked even louder.

"With medication, diet, and exercise, he should be able to control it and live a normal life."

That phrase stuck in my brain. *A normal life.* My father has never lived a normal life. He manages our apartment building, and two others down the street. All three are rent-controlled. Meaning, the rents are so low, the rest of the city hates us. None of the tenants ever wants Dad to enter their apartments. If he sees something illegal—like they moved their boyfriend in over the weekend—he can kick them out. Once someone is out, the landlord can raise the rent. So nobody ever moves. And they usually fix stuff themselves. Which is good because, even though Dad is also considered the building's handyman, he breaks more things than he fixes.

In exchange for taking care of the three small buildings, Dad gets a puny salary and a free three-bedroom apartment. A sweet deal, as far as I can see. We get to live rent-free in Santa Monica, and Dad gets to lie around the house, eating Cheetos—at least when Mom isn't looking.

"No, Gwen," he says to her, "I don't want another heart attack."

"Cardiac *event*," she corrects him.

My mother is shaky in the "normal life" department, too. Last year she announced she was becoming a life coach.

"A huh?" Quinn had asked.

"I'm going to help people fulfill the potential that is life," she said.

"What does that mean, exactly?" I asked.

She brushed a stray hair off her forehead. "You know, the *potential* that is all of our lives. I'm going to help people, you know, fulfill it."

"Who's going to pay you to do that, Gwen?" Dad asked.

"And why would they come to *you*?" I asked. "No offense, Mom. But seriously, why?"

"I'm surrounded by naysayers," she said, marching out of the room. "You'll see. I'll have the last laugh."

It's been a year. So far, Mom hasn't even chuckled. Apparently it's harder than she thought getting friends to cough up money for her attempts to run their lives. Particularly when her own existence seems so tense. It's like my mother grits her teeth through life. Her decision to become a vegetarian, for example. She approached it like she was an alcoholic. One day at a time. Each day, she makes a conscious decision to "just say no" to meat. Don't real vegetarians get a little joy out of their lifestyle? Do they pass a butcher's shop the way a recovering alkie passes a bar?

"Dessert, anyone?" she says hopefully. "Vegan cheese-cake!"

Eight

It's Saturday. D-Day. Drew Day. My heart is pumping so hard my ears are red. Jackie drives, though we take my car. I'm way too nervous to get behind the wheel.

"What is with this mascara?" I say, staring into the visor mirror. "It clumps every time I blink!"

"You look beautiful," Jackie says calmly.

"I look like a drag queen."

Normally, I don't wear makeup—not this much, anyway. Jackie came over early this morning and got a little carried away.

"Blue eyes need lavender shadow," she said. "And your pale skin needs peach blush."

Sitting me down, she brushed and blotted and blended.

Because she'd seen it on a television makeover, she first dabbed shadow and cover stick on the back of her hand. Then, like a Renaissance painter, she used my face as the canvas for her masterpiece.

"Jackie!" I screeched when she held a mirror up to my face. "It's not Halloween!"

Supremely confident, she replied, "It is, however, the day you go from friend to femme fatale. Think you can do that without shadow?"

I believed her. Jackie knew such things. So, I squeezed into my favorite jeans, which were tight because I avoided the three-days-in-a-row horror by wearing a skirt yesterday. On top, I wore a short moss-green cami over a long pink cap-sleeve tee. Very spring chic. Jackie braided two thin strands of my hair—one on either side of my face—and knotted them with a clear bead. Though it was impossible to walk in them comfortably for long, I strapped on my favorite platform sandals, having painted my toenails the night before. Four extra inches of height shaves at least an inch off each thigh. Or so I once read.

Subjectively evaluating my appearance, I came to a conclusion: If I weren't me, and I saw me, I'd think I looked rather sexy. Wobbly and drag-queeny, but sexy.

"Where are we meeting Drew?" Jackie asks, as she pulls into the parking structure on Fourth Street. She's wearing wrinkled chino capris, a white tank, and rubber flip-flops.

"Laying low," she told me earlier. "So Drew is blinded by your beauty."

Jackie's brown hair is knotted into a messy twist. Her tanned arms are smooth and her cheeks are naturally peachy. She's wearing lip gloss. Period. Of course, she looks *fantastic*. She can't help it. If only the football team were with us.

"T-Rex," I say.

As we walk to the meeting site—a huge dinosaur-shaped topiary—I pop on my aviator sunglasses.

"What are you doing?" Jackie asks, alarmed.

"Protecting my eyeballs from second-degree sunburn," I reply.

"Hayley." My best friend sighs impatiently. "Don't you know that your eyes are the windows to your soul? How do you expect Drew to fall at your feet if you won't even let him see your soul?"

She has a point. I think. I'm completely worthless in these matters. At sixteen, I've only kissed a boy once. And frankly, I'm not even sure we really kissed. Jackie was all, "How can you not be sure you kissed?!" But it's true. I was at a slumber party at my cousin's house and I fell asleep. (Which, I stressed to Jackie, you are supposed to do at a *slumber* party.) I awoke in the middle of the night with one of the neighborhood boys pulling himself off my lips. The other girls at the party were not slumbering at all. They'd snuck guys in. I could feel the damp imprint of kiss. But, it was so surreal, it seemed like I dreamed it.

"It doesn't count if you're not awake," Jackie said matter-of-factly.

She'd had major make-out sessions with two boys already—while she was conscious. But Jackie has always been adamant about *not* having a boyfriend.

"Why would I want to tie myself down to one guy?" she always says.

It's the kind of thing you say when you have a choice.

"There he is," Jackie whispers as we near T-Rex. She pulls her sunglasses out of her purse and covers her soul. "He's all yours."

"Hey, Drew," I say, trying to look at him without squinting. Giving him an unobstructed view of my inner depth.

"Hey," he replies. Then he mumbles, "Hey, Jackie."

"Hey," she says, hanging back, looking bored.

"What do you want to do?" I ask Drew.

"Whatever. You?"

"Whatever," I say.

Then the three of us just stand there, in the blazing sun.

"Wanna walk?" he asks.

"Yeah," I say, "let's walk."

We walk. My feet hurt already.

The outdoor Promenade is alive with people. The sun is hot, but the stores rise high enough to create shade on one side. I aim straight for it. I can only look better, I figure, in diminished light. We pass moms pushing strollers and tourists pointing cameras. The yeasty smell of Wetzel's Pretzels mingles with the spicy aroma of Falafel King. I subtly lean close to Drew and inhale his himness. He smells like the ocean. For the first time in my life, I want to strip and go swimming.

"I'm going to check out Abercrombie," Jackie says. "You two go ahead. I'll catch up."

"Um, okay," I say, my heart thudding. She peels off and we're momentarily alone.

"Might as well check out Abercrombie too," Drew says. "Nothing better."

He follows Jackie, and I follow him. When Jackie sees us, she rolls her eyes.

"Can I help you find the right size?" A thin, blond salesgirl instantly pounces on Drew. Somehow making the word *size* sound like porn. I want to pounce on *her*. I'm quite sure I could snap that tiny waist like a breadstick.

"I'm cool," Drew replies. Still, the salesgirl remains glued to his side. She doesn't even see me. I hate this store. Against all laws of science, the bigger you are, the less a salesperson can see you.

"This looks awesome with your eyes," Blondie coos, holding a baby blue shirt up to Drew's chest.

Jackie glares at me from the other side of the store in a "do something" kind of way. So I do.

"Excuse me," I say, holding up a polo shirt. "Do you, um, have this in red?"

"No," she says, barely glancing at me.

"Yellow?" I ask, louder.

"Just what's there," she answers. Then, snottily, she adds, "And only the *sizes* that are there."

My blood instantly boils. Calmly hanging the polo shirt back on the rack, I say, "Oh, I'm sorry. My mistake. This must be Abercrombie and *Bitch*."

Her sappy smile falls as Drew bursts out laughing. Jackie suddenly appears and takes hold of my arm.

"We'll take our business elsewhere," she says. "C'mon, Drew."

Still chuckling, Drew follows us out of the store. Back in the bright sunshine, he says to me, "You're funny."

It's all I can do to stop myself from trotting out every joke I've ever heard and doing a stand-up routine right there on the Promenade. Drew's grin is nearly edible, it's so delicious. I suddenly don't feel hot anymore. I feel warm. The sun is my spotlight.

"Happy to entertain you," I say, trying to inject a little porn-ness into *entertain*. Again, Jackie rolls her eyes, which is getting annoying.

"Let's get out of here," Drew says.

"Yes! Let's!" I nearly shout. "How 'bout a movie? I can get us into whatever we want."

"I have a better idea," he says.

My imagination takes off. The only thing better than a free movie has to be making out. Jackie was *so* right to shovel on the makeup! Drew clearly sees the sexy side of me. He thinks I'm funny, too! How easy was that? But where can we go? My car? Will Jackie quietly get lost? How soon, I wonder, can I remove my shoes without looking like a slut? My feet are already throbbing.

"Follow me," Drew says, turning around.

Giggling sexily, I ask, "Where to?"

He then says the two words that are guaranteed to strike terror in any girl whose talking scale bad-mouths her every morning.

"The beach."

Nine

The beach is nature's practical joke: The Earth is nearly three-fourths ocean, and barely one-fourth of its population looks good in a bathing suit. If even that many. Not to mention sunburn. Why would Mother Nature give us freckles and skin cancer if we're *supposed* to lie practically naked on a beach? It doesn't make sense. Neither does Drew Wyler's suggestion that we swing home to pick up our suits.

"Huh?" I say stupidly, unable to say anything else. What happened to making out in the cool darkness of a movie theater?

"Do either of you have a surfboard?" he asks.

Jackie shoots me a look and I glare at her.

"Uh, no," she says. "No surfboard. Nope. Not at my house."

My best friend is the world's worst liar.

"Doesn't Ty surf?" Drew asks. "I swear I've seen him in the waves."

"Ty?" she stammers. "Waves?"

"Oh, for God's sake," I say, unable to watch Jackie fumble just to save me the mortification of swimwear. "Ty has a surfboard, but we don't. It's his and he won't let us use it. We can go to the beach if you want, but I'm not going home to get my bathing suit and neither is Jackie. It's *Saturday*. The sand will be mobbed. We don't even have towels! The Pier will be even worse. But if you want to go to the beach, we'll go to the beach. Fine."

"Great!" Drew says airily. "Let's go."

Santa Monica State Beach is one of the reasons people move to Southern California. It's also why the jealous want to poison rent-controlled tenants with tofu. The three-and-a-half mile stretch of sand is raked daily. Hunky lifeguards sit high on their towers and flirt with the best boob jobs in LA (the three girls in my school included). You can spot dolphins frolicking off-shore, actors jogging through the surf, wannabe actresses running after them.

All in all, it's an idyllic scene. If you like more than three hundred and forty days of sunshine a year, and water so blue it looks fake.

Me, I like the beach at *night*. Or on the twenty-five days of bad weather. You haven't lived until you've spent Christmas Eve bundled in a woolly sweater, gazing at the black waters of the Pacific. Creepy, but magical.

"Woo hoo!" Drew tears off his shirt and his shoes. He's off and running the moment his bare feet hit the sand.

"Sorry," Jackie says to me, patting one of my cap sleeves. "I know how much you hate sunshine."

Bucking up, I decide to make the best of it. I slip my feet out of my torture sandals and let the hot sand soothe the blisters. I roll my jean cuffs as high as they'll go, and ignore the icky sensation of makeup sliding off my face.

"Woo hoo," I repeat, as Jackie and I join Drew—and most of Santa Monica—at the water's edge.

Jackie, of course, *loves* the beach. She's normal. For my sake, though, she sits on the sand and watches our gear while I pretend to enjoy getting soaked. Drew is body-surfing. I giggle and clap each time he looks my way. I even attempt a mild frolic. But, honestly, I feel like a melted birthday cake. And I'm not sure if dunking my head will improve the makeup situation, or transform my look from Drag Queen to Sad Clown. At least the thick layer of makeup has a high SPF. Doesn't it?

"Sharks are more afraid of you than you are of them," Drew yells.

Just as I'm about to yell something pithy back at him—

not that I can think of anything amusing with my increasingly Sad Clown appearance—I notice that Drew isn't talking to me. He's talking *past* me. To Jackie. I don't hear her respond, but I take it as my cue.

"It's now or never, Hayley," I say out loud. "Strut your stuff."

Looking, I'm sure, like a mother who's diving into the sea to save her drowning baby, I lurch forward into the waves. I'm instantly hit by a whitecap. Then another. I swallow saltwater. Cough my guts up. By the time I flail my way to Drew, I realize he's standing up. I could have gracefully *waded* out to meet him instead of thrashing about like a load of laundry. These are the things you learn the hard way when you go to the beach in daylight.

"The water is fabulous," I say, gasping for air. Then I bite down on my salty tongue. Fabulous? Since when do I use that Hollywood word?

Drew reaches both hands in the water and scoops up the ocean.

"It's life," he says simply. I melt. That's the kind of deep thought a guy who reads Shakespeare for fun has.

As I bob up and down in the surf, I notice that my mouth is hanging open. It's probably due to the fact that Drew is half naked next to me. I can't stop staring at his smooth, bare torso. He has the body of a natural athlete. Not too buff, but defined enough to show that he doesn't spend hours in front of the tube with his hand in an open bag of Cheetos. His light hair is darkened by the water. And I see evidence of an ebbing hairline. Which makes me love him even more.

"Why is Jackie just sitting there?" he asks.

I look ashore as another wave hits the back of my head and topples me headfirst into the breakers. When I resurface, one of my side braids is plastered across my upper lip like a Salvador Dalí moustache.

"She's watching our stuff," I say, tucking my dripping braids behind my ears. A guy like Drew Wyler would never date a girl with a Dalí 'stache. That much I know for sure.

Suddenly, I feel the incredible weight of my wet jeans. My legs have become two anchors. A terrifying thought flashes through my brain. Might I sink right here, unable to keep myself afloat? Will Drew have to lug me to the sand, my neck in the crook of his arm? Will he understand that it's my jeans that weigh so much?

No way am I going to attempt to peel off soaking wet jeans that are as tight as duct tape in front of Drew Wyler. I'd rather drown.

"We can't just leave her there," he says.

"It's okay," I reply, hopping up and down harder. "She hates the ocean."

"Who hates the ocean?" Drew scoffs.

At that moment, he turns and looks at me funny. My heart stops. He's on to me. He knows that *I* hate the ocean. In daylight, anyway. And summer. He's just realized that he's standing in the waves with a freak in skintight wet jeans that weigh fifty pounds. Not to mention a skin-*stretched* body that weighs more than my brother's.

Then, I see the truth. Drew isn't worried that he'll have to lug my ass to shore, he's seen what saltwater and sun can do to makeup. My previous question is answered in the reflection of his horrified stare: I look like a Sad Clown.

"Do you happen to have a mirror on you?" I ask. "I think my nose needs powder."

Drew bursts out laughing. I laugh too. His smile makes me feel light. I'm no longer sinking down to China. I feel positively daring.

"I've been meaning to ask you something," I start, playfully prancing side to side beneath the water.

"Yeah?" he says. Then he dives under a wave and pops back up. "I've been meaning to ask you something, too."

"Really?"

My pulse speeds up. I float. Honestly, I can't feel the bottom of the ocean. Maybe my feet are numb. Maybe it's love.

"You first," I say, smiling coyly.

"No, you," he says.

"No, *you.*"

"No. You."

"Okay." I take a deep breath at the exact moment another wave hits. Saltwater flies down my throat. I cough like a dog choking on a chicken bone. Very unladylike.

Water shoots out of my mouth and nose. Again, about as classy as a belly burp at a funeral. I'm mortified. Drew stands there helplessly.

"Are you okay?" he asks.

Desperate to capture a shred of dignity, I gasp between hacks, "You talk. I'll breathe."

Drew chuckles. Then, he gets serious.

"I was wondering," he says, pausing.

"Yes?" *Cough. Cough.*

"You don't have to answer if you don't want to."

Bark. Bark. "Don't worry. Ask me anything."

He says, "Okay. Here goes."

Beneath the water, my heart is pounding so hard, I'm sure I'm calling whales. The ocean isn't so bad after all. In fact, I feel one with the cradle of evolution. I, too, shall emerge from the sea a new species—a girl with a boyfriend.

"What is it, Drew?" I manage to ask in my sexiest voice.

"Do you think Jackie would go out with me?"

I blink. My eyelashes are sticky.

"What?"

"Jackie. Do you think she'd go out with me?"

It's just a nanosecond, but I literally feel the Earth stop turning. A slight jolt, like tapping the brakes of a car. In that fraction of a second—so quick, it can't be measured—I feel my world change.

Drew has the sweetest look on his face. His eyes show more white, his lips are curved in hope. He looks the way my brother, Quinn, looked when he asked me to hold him while he learned how to ice-skate.

It's a face you have to protect.

"She never hooks up with just one guy," I say. The first sentence in my brand-new world.

Drew exhales. "That's cool," he says.

"I'll talk to her."

Drew leans over and plants a salty, wet kiss on my cheek. It feels just like that. Salty. Wet. A cheek kiss that will never be any other kind.

"Thanks, Hayley. You're a true friend."

Ten

Of course Drew likes Jackie. Everyone likes Jackie. How could I not have seen it?

I sigh. Feel a sharp ache in my chest.

The truth, of course, is that I *did* see it. I always see it. Only I didn't want to see it this time. For once, I wanted my eyes to deceive me. This time, I longed to be the chosen one.

"I have to go," I say abruptly.

Even though we're both soaking wet, standing there in the Pacific Ocean, I don't want to risk Drew seeing me cry. So, I bite down on the inside of my cheek and wade to shore.

"Wait!" he calls after me.

Turning, I gaze at his beautiful, glistening chest.

"What were you going to ask me?" he shouts.

A wave slams against my waist. This time, it doesn't knock me over. Inhaling, I lift my head and yell, "Is it true? What you said?"

Drew looks confused. "About what?"

"Sharks. Are they really more afraid of us than we are of them?"

He laughs. For a moment I let myself drown in the hollows of his cheeks. Then I feel tears gather in my whole head, so I fall face-first into the water. And Drew laughs some more.

Jackie knows better.

"What's wrong?" she asks, alarmed, when I join her on the sand.

"I'm getting sunburned," I say. "I want to go home."

She puts her hand on my wet shoulder. "Did something happen?"

"No."

"You sure?"

"You want a ride or not?" I snap.

We gather our stuff, leaving Drew in the water and his shirt and shoes on the beach. My wet jeans weigh a ton. Each step feels like I'm dragging a yule log across the sand. My nose runs; my bare feet burn. My brain is shooting sparks. Jackie, normally a motormouth, doesn't say a word the whole way. By the time we get to my car behind the

43

Promenade, I'm almost dry. Jackie rests her hand gently on my shoulder and says, "Whenever you're ready to talk about it, I'm ready to listen."

My lips pressed tightly together, I nod. Then I drive her home. The moment she gets out of the car, I wave, press my right foot on the gas pedal, and let the tears tumble over my bottom lids.

Of course Drew likes Jackie. How could you not?

As I drive east on the Santa Monica Freeway, I can barely see anything at all. My eyes are blurry with hot tears. Each time I blink them away, the tide rises again. Good thing I'm in traffic—of course. This is LA. There is always traffic. The word *free*way is a joke. But today, I don't care. Even if it means slowly inching away, I'm glad to be out of there.

I drive past the curved off-ramps of the San Diego Freeway, staring out through the smog to the ugly neighborhoods on either side. Past a used car dealership. A mall. Finally, Robertson Boulevard feels far enough. No one knows me here. I can be invisible. I exit the freeway and enter Culver City. At Venice Boulevard, I find what I'm looking for. The lunchtime crowd is already eating. Good, I say to myself. The ovens will be hot. I won't have to wait long.

The aroma of garlic and tomato sauce assaults me the moment I walk through the glass door. One person is ahead of me in line.

Perfect.

Flipping open my phone, I pretend to make a call. I wait for my pretend friends to pretend pick up.

"Hi," I say into my dead phone. "I'm at the pizza place. What kind do you want?"

As I fake listen, I scan the menu. My mouth waters. My stomach gurgles. My heart aches.

"Pepperoni?" I say loudly. "Large?"

When it's my turn to order, I hold up one finger and say into the phone, "Large pepperoni pizza, right? And a liter of Coke?"

Pausing, I nod. Then I say, "See you soon," before flipping my phone shut.

"Sorry," I say to the guy behind the counter. "My friends can never make up their minds."

"It's cool," he says, shrugging.

While my pizza cooks, I sit at an empty table near the window. Culver City looks like every other LA town—flat, brown, full of cars. There's a college here, and an independent film studio. Some of the city is pretty nice. But, from my current vantage point, I could be anywhere. Which is exactly what I want. To disappear.

As soon as the pizza is ready, I pay and practically run out the door. I ask for four cups for the Coke, though I know I'll swig it directly from the bottle. Intellectually, I *know* the counter guy doesn't care who I am or how many people will be eating this pizza. Emotionally, though, I can't bear for him to know the truth. I can't even stand to know the truth myself.

On autopilot, I do what I've done dozens of times before. With the hot pizza box on the passenger seat, I pull out of the parking lot in search of a place to hide. My heart is racing. My palms are damp. I can hardly wait. I look for a tree, or a back alley. No smelly Dumpsters. No pedestrians. After roaming the residential streets off National, I see a space meant just for me. It's in front of a house under construction. The workmen are all at lunch. There *is* a Dumpster, but it's filled with Sheetrock. No stink. A good place to toss the evidence when I'm through.

Pulling over, I kill the engine. My hand trembles as I open the box lid and release the spicy steam. As I take my first bite, I feel the melted cheese ooze across the roof of my mouth. The salty pepperoni excites my tongue. I swallow fast, take another big bite. Eyes closed, I lean against the headrest and chew. My tense body relaxes. I have my fix.

Within fifteen minutes, the pizza box is full of crusts. The liter of Coke is half empty. I'm stuffed. I only tasted the first bite or two. The rest was inhaled as if I were in a trance. Quickly, I swing open the car door and toss the garbage in the Dumpster. I can't stand to see any reminder of what I've just done.

But I *feel* it.

My stomachache is stronger than my heartache. For now.

"Hayley, you jerk," I say out loud.

46

I hate myself. I want to throw up, but I don't. I won't let myself go down that road. Instead, I start my car, pull out, and aim for home. Praying my mother won't smell the failure on my breath.

Eleven

Mom is just returning from the gym when I get home.

"Ah," she says, "is there anything more satisfying than sweat?"

"I can think of a hundred things," I say. Passing her, I add, "A hundred and *one* if you count deodorant."

"Aren't you the funny girl." Mom playfully pinches my chin.

Funny girl. Those two words pierce my heart like an ice pick to the chest. That's what I am. A funny girl. A *friend*. Nobody's girlfriend. The girl with the pretty *face*.

Stomping down the hallway to my room, I slam the door behind me. Both physically and mentally, I feel as though I'm going to explode. My phone is beeping. Jackie has gone text-crazy. But I don't want to talk to her. I don't want to talk to anyone. I want to lie facedown on my bed until the hollows of Drew Wyler's cheekbones are erased from my brain forever.

"Hayley!" Mom yells down the hall. I don't answer. My full stomach bulges out over my jeans. I feel the top button press into my flesh. I need a shower. I smell like seawater and tomato sauce. No way can I bear to see myself naked, though. Not yet. Not ever.

"Hayley!"

She won't stop. It's easier to give in.

"What?" I lift my mouth off my pillow and yell back at her.

"We're having an early dinner," she bellows. "Come help me grate the carrots."

Groaning, I bellow back, "I'm not hungry."

In a flash, my mother is in my room.

"What did you eat?" she demands.

"Nothing," I say.

"Nothing? You have to eat, Hayley. I'm making carrot and parsnip curry."

"I ate a big lunch," I say. "I'm not hungry."

Mom sits on my bed. I turn my face to the wall.

"What did you eat today, Hayley?" she asks firmly.

"A salad," I say. "A big salad."

She puts her warm hand on my back and says, "Why do I smell pepperoni?"

I sigh. My mother was a drug-sniffing beagle in a previous life. She can smell processed meat a mile away.

"It was an *antipasto* salad," I say weakly. But I know I'm already doomed.

"Honey," she says softly, "if you won't see Dr. Weinstein, at least come to a meeting with me. I'm going tomorrow morning. You don't have to do anything but watch. If you hate it, you never have to come back."

At the worst possible moment, a pepperoni burp leaps up my windpipe. I clamp my lips shut and bury my face in my pillow. My eyes and nose sting like crazy as the burp escapes through my nostrils. Few things are more aromatic than a pepperoni burp. A sausage burp, maybe. Or a raw garlic hiccup. But a pepperoni burp almost leaves a stain on the wall—it's that powerful. There's no mistaking it for something vegetarian.

Mom pats my back. I don't have to look. I know she's covering her nose with her free hand.

"If I go, will you leave me alone?" I say, my face still concealed in my now-stinking pillow.

"Yes," she says. Though I know she's lying.

"What time is the meeting?" I ask.

"Ten thirty."

"Okay," I say. "I'll go."

I'm lying, too. Tomorrow morning, I'll get up early and be out of the house by nine.

"Great!" Mom kisses the back of my head. "You won't be

sorry, Hayley. Changing your life is the most exciting thing you can do."

What about vanishing into thin—or in my case, *fat*—air? Could anything be better than that?

Jackie is as persistent as my mother. She calls, e-mails, texts, IMs. Soon she'll be at my front door. I know her. In a previous life, Jackie was a bulldog.

Finally, I text her back. I can't yet trust my voice not to quiver over the phone.

"Hi," I write.

A string of exclamation points instantly fills my screen.

"Needed some quiet tm," I write.

"WHT HAPPND???!!!!!!"

Like ripping a Band-Aid off, I decide not to prolong the agony.

"Drew likes u."

Ouch. The fresh scab comes with it.

"WHT????"

"He wants to ask u out," I write.

As I stare at the text screen in my hand, waiting for her response, my phone rings. I let it ring four times before answering.

"Please leave a message at the beep," I say into the phone, my voice only slightly quivery.

"Hayley—"

"Beep!"

"Hayley."

I can't say anything.

"You don't have to talk," Jackie says. "But please listen. I'm *so* sorry. Honestly, I barely know the guy. I never did anything to encourage him. Nothing. I swear."

"I know," I say.

"God, Hayley. How unbelievably awful."

This is why I love my best friend. Only Jackie would think Drew's desire for her is an unbelievably awful event.

"What did you say to him?" she asks me.

"I told him I'd talk to you."

"What?! Why?"

"I don't want you biting his head off when he asks you out."

"No way would I ever—"

"He's a good guy, Jackie."

More silence. I can't believe what I just said any more than Jackie can believe what she just heard. Am I giving her the green light? Do I *want* my best friend to hook up with the boy who just broke my heart? Surprised by my own maturity, I flash on what Mom said to me. Maybe changing your life *is* the most exciting thing you can do.

"Not right away, okay?" I say quietly. "Give me a couple of weeks to heal the gaping hole in my aorta."

"Are you serious?" Jackie asks.

I ask myself the same question. Maybe it's the pepperoni talking, but I think so.

"Why shouldn't the two people I love hang out together?"

I hear Jackie breathing over the phone line. I can almost hear her mind clicking, too. Thinking back, I'm quite sure I saw a spark in her eyes the moment we both first saw Drew Wyler. When he arrived at Pacific High, it was impossible to miss him. He had this studied scruffiness that made me flush. I could tell he was smart, too. His eyes took in everything before his mouth opened.

"Dibs," I'd said to Jackie.

She had laughed. It was the first time I'd ever marked a boy as mine. Last year, it didn't matter. Neither one of us had any classes with him. This year, though, I lost my breath when I walked into AP English and saw him sitting there. My knees collapsed into the seat next to him and I thought of nothing else but getting his laser eyes to zero in on me. How could I have been so deluded as to think they would?

"No way, Hayley," Jackie says over the phone. "Never. Not ever. It's not going to happen. If Drew Wyler asks me out, I'm going to turn him down in three languages. No, *non, nyet.*"

Now I burst into tears.

"Thank *God!*" I sob.

Twelve

Isn't pride one of the seven deadly sins? I seem to remember that from my attempt to impress Drew by slogging through Dante's levels of hell. (Clearly, it didn't work.) My own hell is waiting for me at the front door this morning.

"Did you really think you could fool me?" Mom asks.

"I was just going jogging," I say. "I'll be back in time for your stupid meeting."

She throws her head back and releases a witch cackle.

"Since I knew you'd try to skip out early, I lied about the meeting time. It's at *nine* thirty. Ha, ha, *ha*."

Damn. Trapped. I stifle the urge to gnaw my own leg off and escape—hopping—to my car.

"It'll be fun, honey," Mom says cheerfully. "Now, let's go."

The Waist Watcher meeting room is on the third floor of an office building on Wilshire Boulevard. Mom snatches my hand as I reach for the elevator button.

"Never ride when you can walk," she chirps. "Never walk when you can jog. Never jog when you can—"

"Got it," I say, wishing I could sprint my ass right out of there. Instead, I plod up the stairs behind my mother, who prances ahead of me like a gazelle.

"Gwen!" Inside the meeting room, a greeter with dyed black hair hugs my mother. "How was your week?"

"Quarter pound loss, ten gram increase in fiber!"

I audibly groan.

"And, I've brought my daughter, Hayley!"

"I'm not fat," I say. "I'm just too short for my weight."

Shoe Polish Head smiles condescendingly and hugs me too. Her perfume sticks to my clothes. The smell mingles with the other odor in the room: fat people taking off their shoes.

"Welcome!"

I force a smile. Does everyone here talk in exclamation points?

Mom joins the line of chubbettes in socks. She's the thinnest person in the room. No wonder she likes to come to these meetings! The woman ahead of her is so bottom-heavy she looks like a bowling pin. The man at the end of the line, in cut-off sweatpants, has the wrinkled knees of an aging elephant. One by one, they disappear behind a screen.

When they emerge, they either flash a thumbs-up or avoid eye contact.

"I'll be over there," I say, pointing to an empty chair across the room.

"Keep me company," Mom replies. "I'll only be a minute."

To my utter mortification, Mom disappears behind the screen, then lets out a loud "Wahoo!" Upon her exit, she does the "happy dance" I've seen her do when Quinn gets an A or I agree to an afternoon of Mom Bonding.

"I made my goal weight!" she squeals.

The Elephant Man claps. Others in line cheer, but I can't look. Is my mother as dense as a post? Most of these people are so far from their goal, they're not even on the field.

"Fiber rocks!" Mom says as I practically run to the other side of the room.

The meeting lasts half an hour, but it feels like half a week. As it turns out, Shoe Polish Head is the leader.

"For the benefit of the newbies," she says, looking directly at me, "I've lost seventy-three pounds, and have kept it off for five years."

The group applauds as the woman produces a blown-up photo of her former blown-up body. I'm impressed with her success. Still, I can't help but notice she could stand to lose fifty more.

"Summer is just around the corner," she continues, "and we all know what that means. Bikinis!"

I burst out laughing. Honestly, I thought she was making a joke. Mom glares at me as the leader marches on.

"Who wants to share any successes or challenges over the past week?"

Several hands go up.

"Theresa?"

An older woman, with two cumulus clouds for upper arms, begins.

"Last weekend was my son's wedding."

Collectively, the crowd moans in sympathy.

"Honestly," Theresa says, "the mini egg rolls were calling to me all night!"

A room full of double chins nods.

"At my daughter's wedding," a woman says, "it was the smoked salmon toast points. I couldn't stop myself."

"What about the cake?" someone yells.

The whole group groans and shares stories about the many cakes that have whispered in their ears.

I feel queasy. Is this where I'm headed? Will appetizers call *my* name? Will cakes mock me? Will my life become a series of numbers? Fat grams, calories, pounds, exercise minutes? Will I get more turned on by fiber than by my own husband?

Another woman raises her hand to ask if anyone knows how many Waist Watcher units are in a Peep (she still has several of the marshmallowy chicks in her freezer from Easter). As the debate begins, I seize the opportunity to stand and run from the room. I don't stop until I can't run anymore.

Not surprisingly, I find myself near Jackie's place.

"Wanna see a movie?" I ask her, panting.

"Cool," she says.

Before we leave for the Cineplex, I call my dad to tell him I won't be home all day. Not even for dinner.

"Okay," he says. Dad never asks any questions.

In the dark movie theater, with a large buttery popcorn on my lap, I sink into the soft seat and let myself evaporate into the screen. I become the actress who gets the guy. I wear her clothes, feel the freedom of her body. Until Jackie whispers, "Are you okay?" I don't even notice the tears streaming down my cheeks.

It's dark when I get home.

"Hayley?"

Mom's voice calls from the living room. The house is eerily quiet. Quinn must be playing a video game in his room.

"Sorry I ran off, Mom," I shout, on my way to my room.

"Can you please come in here for a moment?"

A shiver stops me. Her voice is weird.

"Everything okay?" I ask.

"Just come in here," Mom says.

My heart thudding, I circle back and pass through the double French doors into the living room. Mom is sitting there. So is Dad. The television is off.

"What's wrong?" I ask.

"Sit down."

I sit.

"Your father and I have been having a serious discussion," Mom begins, sighing.

Tears instantly well up in my eyes. "Are you getting a divorce?" I ask.

"No," Mom replies, scoffing. "We've been talking about *you.*"

My tears dry. Instead, my palms get wet.

"What *about* me?" I ask.

"We're worried about you," Dad says.

"Why? I'm *fine.*"

"It's your weight, honey," Mom says.

I leap to my feet. "God, Mom. When will you get off my back?!"

"You're absolutely right," she says.

My mouth falls open. I stand there and blink.

"Your father and I think that, right now, I may be doing more harm than good."

Dad leans forward. "We've been talking to a therapist," he says. "She thinks you may be under too much pressure right now. Body image pressure."

"Hello? I live in Southern California, where there are

more gym memberships than library cards. Yeah! I guess I am under a teensy bit of pressure."

"How would you like a break this summer?" Mom asks.

"I am *not* going to a fat camp!" I shout.

"We had something else in mind," Dad says gently. "Do you remember Patrice?"

"Mom's friend Patty?" I ask.

My mother nods. "She calls herself Patrice now."

I remember Patty—Patrice—very well. We met when I was a kid, but I've seen her a couple of times since then. Mom and Patrice were best friends in college. I remember thinking the ungenerous thought that Patrice was way too cool to be my mom's friend. So cool, in fact, that she married an Ita—

"Patrice has a big house in Umbria," Mom says. "She's invited you to visit for the summer."

"Is this a joke, Mom? Because I left the Waist Watcher meeting?"

My mother stands and walks over to me. "It's no joke. The therapist thinks you need a change of scenery. So I called Patrice. Her kids are younger than you, but she's happy to have you."

I'm speechless.

Behind my back, my parents have been slamming me to a therapist. My own mother is pawning me off to babysit foreign kids all summer. Jackie will be a continent and an ocean away from me . . . mere miles from Drew. I don't speak the language. I don't like meeting new people. And I have no idea where Umbria is . . .

Who cares?!

I'm going to Italy!

Thirteen

"You can't go to Italy!"

It's Monday morning. School is out in two weeks. Jackie is in the passenger seat as I drive us to Pacific High. The same route I always take. But this morning, everything is different.

"How can you go to *Italy*?" my best friend says, near tears.

I was going to call her last night, but it wasn't real yet. My parents' lips moved when they spoke about my trip, but their words didn't penetrate my brain. I kept blinking and staring. Who are these people? I don't have the kind of parents who send their child to Europe.

"Ty was going to teach us how to night-surf!" Jackie whines.

"I never agreed to that," I say.

"But I had all summer to talk you into it!"

Ever since my real parents were cloned and started saying stuff like, "A summer in Italy will be an asset on your college apps," and "You're old enough to spend time on your own," I've felt like I was airlifted into someone else's life. Is this a new reality show? *Hayley's Dream.* Will I wake up to a lunch invitation at the Olive Garden instead of a plane ticket to Rome?

"I'm going to miss you horribly," Jackie says, sniffing.

"Me, too," I reply, suddenly realizing that we'll be apart for ten long weeks.

"It's worse for me," Jackie says. "I'm the one being left."

I can't help thinking that I'd rather stay in Santa Monica and be with Drew than fly to Italy and be alone. But it's a moot point. I'll be alone no matter which continent I'm on. Loveless with my pretty face.

Jackie hears me sigh.

"Have a good time," she says reluctantly.

"I'll try."

"But not *so* good that you fall completely in love with Italy and never come back."

"Impossible," I say, grinning. "It's too hot."

"Okay," she says, "then promise me you won't visit the Italian Alps or Germany or Switzerland or any of the cooler countries nearby."

Laughing out loud, I promise.

Pulling into the Pac High student lot, I park and check my hair in the rearview mirror. As I gaze into my gray-blue eyes, I see a girl on the edge of a cliff. It's a grassy, jade-green precipice, high above a sea of smooth, sapphire-blue water. Her sheer dress blows in the breeze; she is barefoot. Ten toes curl over the edge. Her heart thumps. She's scared. Will she fly, or fall like a rock?

"I'll e-mail you every day," I say, reaching across the seat to hug my best friend before she can see the tears welling in my eyes.

"Hey," Drew says, when I sit next to him in English class.

I'm wearing my favorite outfit—old jeans and a new lacy white shirt. My hair is up and my sandals are flat. It's about comfort now, even as I feel totally uncomfortable next to the boy who broke my heart. I don't want to see him. I want to pretend we never went to the beach. I don't want to look in his eyes and see his desire for someone else.

"Hey," I say back.

Quickly, I pull a book out of my pack and bury my head in it. Still, I can feel his gaze on me. I know what he wants to know. *Did you talk to her?*

"Have you chosen your summer book yet?" I ask, glancing up.

Let him wait.

"I'm thinking *Catch-22*," he says. "Or *No Exit*."

I nod and swallow the lump in my throat. I'm familiar

with both feelings. Drew tucks his hair behind his ear. His right leg, I notice, is bobbing up and down. He seems nervous. Beside him, I wish I could disappear.

"Open your journals, class," Ms. Antonucci says. "This morning I want you to write a ten-minute essay on the color red."

"You mean a scarlet letter?" I quip.

Everyone laughs. Except Drew. Ignoring his stare, I pull my journal out of my backpack and open to a fresh page.

"Ready?" Ms. Antonucci says. "Go."

Taking a deep breath, I leap.

"Red," I write, "is the color of *life*. It's blood, passion, rage. It's menstrual flow and afterbirth. Beginnings and violent end. Red is the color of love. Beating hearts and hungry lips. Roses, Valentines, cherries. Red is the color of shame. Crimson cheeks and spilled blood. Broken hearts, opened veins. A burning desire to return to white."

I stop and look up. My heart feels heavy. My eyes sting. Will I ever know the passion of red? Will a boy's hungry lips ever seek mine?

"You finished, Hayley?" Ms. Antonucci asks.

"Yeah," I say, putting my pen down. Then I close my journal and wait for the rest of the class to catch up.

Fourteen

Somehow, miraculously, it's here. The last day of school. I feel both excited and hollow—looking ahead and behind with each beat of my heart. Tomorrow, I say good-bye to everything and everyone I know. Even my language! Will I make friends in Italy? Will they think I'm an obese American? *Am* I obese? What's the cut-off weight?

"*Ciao*, Hayley." It's what I've been writing in yearbooks. Not that I sign that many. Unlike Jackie, who practically has carpal tunnel syndrome.

"Memorize every moment," Ms. Antonucci writes in my book. A week ago, when I told her about my summer in Italy, she sighed and said, "Ah, the best food in the world."

Inside, I groaned. That's all I need—a fattening summer.

Quietly, Ms. Antonucci leaned toward me and added, "Open yourself up to everything you're going to experience, Hayley. Don't hold back."

I'm not sure what she meant and, honestly, it freaked me out a little. Was she talking about food? Opening myself up to spaghetti and meatballs? Does she have any idea what kind of feral monster would be unleashed if I didn't clutch the reins of my appetite for dear life?

"Yeah, okay," I said, even though I'd already formulated an entirely different plan. The moment I land on Italian soil, I'm going to hold *on*. If I eat less than a thousand calories a day, I'll come home thirty pounds lighter. Instead of a summer *abroad*, I'll have a summer a*thin*. Without my mother breathing down my neck, it ought to be easy. Patrice is cool. She won't smell my breath for sulfites.

"Hey."

With his hands jammed into his front pockets, Drew suddenly appears in the quad. My heart instantly bounces into my throat. I've successfully avoided him for the past two weeks. I even changed my seat in English class, pretending that I needed glasses and couldn't see the chalkboard. What I could see, however, was the hurt in his eyes. Like he was my brother ice-skating alone.

Now I can't look him in the eye.

"What's up?" I ask, glancing over his shoulder.

Drew gets close, and my cheeks flush. Which really pisses me off. When your brain knows it's over, how long does it take the rest of your body to get the message?

He just stares at me. Doesn't say a word. He doesn't have to.

I look down at my feet.

"I've been meaning to talk to you," I say, not at all convincingly.

The muscles in his cheeks bulge in and out. His black eyes jab my soul.

"About Jackie," I add.

"What about her?" he asks.

I have no idea what to say. I can't tell him the truth and he'll know instantly if I lie.

"What about her?" Drew repeats, with a definite edge to his voice.

I'm back on the cliff. My toes grip the edge and my heart thumps so hard it hurts.

Don't hold back, Hayley.

"What the hell," I say.

I leap.

"Jackie is going to be all sad this summer because I'm gone. Though she doesn't know it yet, she'd like it if you called her. She'll say no if you ask her out, but keep asking. She wants you to. Trust me."

Inhaling, I add, "I want you to, also."

Drew's lips bend up in a smile. "Thanks," he says simply. Then he turns and walks away. I watch him grow smaller, burning the image of his back on my brain.

All of a sudden, he turns around.

"Hayley!"

"Yeah?"

"Ciao."

Fifteen

I've quit my job and packed my suitcase. I have a passport, three hundred euros, and an ATM card in a travel wallet Dad bought me that hangs around my neck. I also have a downloaded photo of Patrice. Not that I'll need it. I'm sure she'll instantly recognize the American girl in tight Levis with a panicked look on her face.

My plane leaves at six p.m., flies all night, and arrives in London at noon—British time—the next day. From London's Heathrow Airport, I catch a two-fifteen plane to Rome, where Patrice will meet me. Factoring in the different time zones, I'll be traveling twenty-four hours straight. It's the most grown-up thing I've ever done. I'm still in shock that my parents are sending me away for the summer.

Even if a professionally licensed therapist suggested it. A professionally licensed facialist once suggested a light chemical peel to get rid of my freckles and Mom was, like, *horrified*.

Earlier this morning she went through my suitcase and pulled out the stuff I *won't* need.

My phone. (No cell service.)

My keys. (She'll let me in the apartment when I get home.)

My favorite pullover sweater. (Italy is hot.)

She also found the Milky Way bars I'd stashed in the zippered pocket.

"Hayley," she said disapprovingly.

"They're Milky Way *Minis*, Mother."

Clucking, she confiscated them. I made a mental note to check the trash cans before we left.

All day, I was in a daze. I know I should feel ecstatic, but too much has happened too fast. My brain is like my metabolism—sluggish when required to work overtime. The skin on my cheeks is tingling, and it's almost like my ears are packed with cotton balls. I hear everyone, but they're muffled.

"Francesco Totti," Quinn says.

"Wha—?"

"God, Hayley," Quinn screeches at me. "I've told you a million times! He's my favorite soccer player. Will you *please* buy me his jersey or get me his autograph? *God.*"

I roll my eyes. "Can't you follow football like a normal American boy?"

Mom steps out of the kitchen and hands me a brown bag. "For the plane," she says.

I peer inside, take a whiff. "No way am I bringing a Tofurky sandwich to Italy!"

"I added avocado," she says, in a singsong way.

Dad, behind her, shoots me a smile-now-and-throw-it-away-later look.

I smile. I'll throw the sandwich away when I retrieve my Milky Way candy bars. I mean, Milky Way *Minis*.

"We leave in half an hour," Dad says. "If anyone has to go to the bathroom, start now."

I don't have to pee, but there is something I *do* have to do.

"I'll be right back," I say.

"Hayley!"

"Don't worry, Dad. I'll be home in time."

Before either parent can stop me, I open the door to our apartment, dash down the hallway, and run out of the building.

Immediately, I'm blinded by the white sunlight. Will Italy be this brain-blastingly bright? Squinting, I keep my head down and jog the whole way to Jackie's.

"I have to talk to you," I say, panting, as she opens the front door to her house.

"You're not going to Italy?!" Jackie's eyes light up.

"I'm going."

She groans. "Come in."

We said our good-byes last night. Both crying, we realized that we'd spoken to each other nearly every day for the past five years. We've talked about nothing, everything, anything. Yet, today, before I leave for the summer, I need to mention one more thing.

"Sit down," I say.

"Sit down? Uh-oh. Are you going to vote me off the island?"

"It's important."

Jackie sits. Her eyebrows bunch up in concern.

"Don't say anything until I'm finished, okay?" I say.

She nods. I inhale hard, blow it out, then begin.

"You're my best friend. I love you. I want you to have a great summer. And I want you to go out with Drew if y—"

"No way, Hayley!"

"Let me finish."

Jackie pouts and presses her lips shut with her first two fingers.

"Drew likes you, and I know you'll never even look at him because of me. So, that's what I came here to say. He's a really good guy. Even if nothing ever happens between you two, I know he'd never like me more than a friend. So, what I'm saying is, it's okay with me if you hang out with him this summer. I'm giving you the green light."

Jackie stares at me and blinks.

"Okay?" I ask.

"May I talk now?"

"I'm all ears."

"I have no interest in Drew Wyler. He's nice enough, I mean, for a wonk. But that whole bookish, monosyllabic type doesn't do it for me. As you know, I'm holding out for Wentworth Miller. Though I'm still not sure what I'll call him. Wenty? Worthy? Anyway, thanks for the green light, Hayley, but Wenty and I will take a pass. Or is it Worthy and I . . . ?"

I laugh. "It's okay to change your mind."

"I won't," Jackie says. "Now go. Before I change my mind about throwing myself in front of your parents' car so they can't drive you to the airport."

Sixteen

The International Terminal in the Los Angeles Airport was renamed Tom Bradley International Terminal a few years ago in honor of the mayor. But nobody calls the LA airport anything but LAX. Not *lax*, but L-A-X.

Since I have to check in two hours before my flight leaves, and there will probably be traffic on the freeway, Dad decreed that we leave our house by three. By three fifteen, my whole family is in the car.

"Seriously," I say as Dad pulls away from the curb. "Everybody doesn't have to wait with me."

"Of course we'll wait with you!" Mom says. "You think we're just going to drop you off?"

"A girl can dream," I mutter under my breath.

Dad says, "Those parking rates *are* atrocious, Gwen."

Ignoring him, Mom turns to me in the backseat. "Do you realize, sweetie, you're the first of my offspring to leave the United States?"

"Quinn is *twelve*, Mom. Don't you need pubic hair before you're allowed to leave the country?"

Quinn socks my arm.

Mom warns, "Don't say words like *pubic*, Hayley, when you're with Patrice. I want her to see that I raised a lady."

"You did raise a lady," I reply. "You should feel Quinn's girly-man punch."

Quinn socks my arm *hard*.

"Ow," I say.

"Knock it off back there," Dad calls over his shoulder. "Enjoy these hairless years, Quinn. By the time you're my age, hair starts sprouting out of your ears."

"Ewwww," my brother and I both moan.

"If I remember correctly," Mom says wistfully, "Italian women don't shave their armpits. Or their legs."

"But they *do* shave their moustaches," Dad says, chuckling.

Quinn adds, "Did you bring your razor, Hayley?"

"You're just jealous because I *have* hair to shave," I reply.

By the time we get to the airport, the family banter has deteriorated into vague grumbles. We're all sweaty and cranky. My father refuses to run the car's air conditioner unless we're in the first stages of heatstroke. Which we probably are.

"Air-conditioning is bad for the environment," Dad says, every time we complain. But he's not fooling anyone. The moment gas prices surged over two bucks a gallon, my father became an avid conservationist of the environment inside his *wallet*.

We circle the airport twice looking for an open parking meter. Grudgingly, Dad gives up and pulls into the lot.

"Highway robbery," he grunts.

The moment I step out into it, the ninety-degree heat in the parking lot presses hard against me. I feel like I'm being ironed. At least I'm out of the car swamp. Red-faced and damp, my family trudges to the terminal from the farthest edge of the lot, where Mom insisted we park.

"Hayley is going to be sitting still all night," she said. "She needs exercise. We all do."

"Wouldn't I be lying down, asleep in my bed, if I were home?" I asked.

Mom made a *pffft* sound and said, "Just walk. Briskly."

So we're walking. Not briskly at all. Dad rubs his shoulder as he pulls my rolling bag. Mom annoyingly jogs circles around us. Quinn slaps his feet on the pavement and pops gum in my ear. I thought I would feel a tug of sadness at leaving my family for the whole summer, but surprisingly I don't.

"Last chance to leave me at the curb," I chirp hopefully. But everyone clomps inside.

Mercifully, the airline terminal is air-conditioned. My

sweat quickly turns to ice water on my face. Even more mercifully, only ticketed passengers are allowed beyond the security checkpoint. The last remnants of family bonding will be used up in the snaking line leading up to the ticketing agent.

"At Patrice's, remember to be the first one up after dinner so you can clear the plates," Mom says. "And make your bed every day. I mean it, Hayley. *Every* day."

"I won't embarrass you, Mom. Can you promise me the same?"

"Don't get fresh."

At last, it's my turn to check in.

"Has your suitcase been in your possession the whole time?" the airline employee asks me.

"No," I say.

She looks up. "Where has it been?"

"In my father's hands."

She sighs. "This question is designed to determine if a stranger has slipped anything into your luggage."

"Oh. No. Though my mother may have slipped in a bag of baby carrots. There's no stopping her."

The clerk smiles. "You're all set," she says, handing me my baggage claim check and boarding pass. "Gate number eleven."

With my carry-on tote slung over my shoulder, I'm ready to go.

"Security may take a while," I say. "I should get in the line."

Reluctantly, Mom nods. She bites her lip and reaches into her purse for a tissue.

Dad hugs me and says, "Be a good girl, hon."

Quinn says, "See ya," and blows a huge bubble that pops on his face.

Taking the mature road, I stifle a laugh and turn to hug my mother good-bye.

"Wait!" she shrieks. Spinning on her heels, Mom dashes for the nearest newsstand.

"I already have *People* magazine!" I call after her. But she doesn't listen. What else is new? Five minutes later, my mother scurries back to us with a huge bottle of water.

"Hydrate massively before you get on the plane," she says to me, breathless.

"Security will only confiscate it," I say.

"Drink it while you're in line, then."

I scoff. "Why did I get a seat assignment when I'll be spending the whole flight in the bathroom?"

"I'm serious, Hayley. Airline travel sucks all the moisture from your body. If you don't replenish, you'll pay a steep price."

Dad says, "Speaking of steep prices, if we spend another ten minutes here, the parking rate goes up ten bucks."

"Bye, Mo—" Before I can stop her, my mother grabs my carry-on tote and unzips it.

"I'll just put your water bottle in . . . Hayley!"

"I'll miss you so much," I say, quickly throwing my arms

around her while I attempt to close the tote. "You're the best mother ev—"

"Hayley, Hayley, Hayley."

Busted.

I hang my head as Mom pulls out the Milky Way bars I rescued from the trash. Then, she vainly searches my tote for the brown bag she gave me earlier.

"Did you even *try* the Tofurky sandwich?" she asks, shaking her head.

"No," I mumble.

"It's too late to order a special vegetarian meal for the plane!"

"They are Milky Way *Minis*, Gwen," Dad offers, trying to help. "Give her a break. It's a long flight."

Quinn sneers. "God, Hayley. You eat garbage."

"Shut up, you hairless twerp," I snap.

"Okay." Mom takes a deep breath to settle herself. "No damage has been done yet. We caught it in time."

Staring into my eyes, she says, "Tell me honestly, honey, is there any other contraband in your carry-on luggage?"

"Other than my crack vials?"

"This is no time to joke. You're embarking on a journey that will change your life. If you *let* it. I only want you to start off on the right foot."

Sticking my right foot out, I say, "I'm ready, Mom. Give me back my bag. I promise to hydrate. Take away my candy bars. Dunk me in holy water, if you have to.

Just let me go, okay?"

Again, Mom bites her lip. "You know there's a food court in there, don't you? Have you established a plan of attack? What are you going to do when a Big Mac calls your name?"

"Mom!"

"Ka-ching, ka-ching," Dad says, pointing to his watch.

"I have to go to the bathroom," Quinn adds.

Dad glares at him. "Didn't you go at home?"

Quinn doesn't answer, just crosses his legs.

"I'm going to be fine," I say, gently pulling my tote out of her vise grip. "I won't talk to strangers or Big Macs."

"How do you say *McDonald's* in Italian?" Quinn asks. "McDonaldo?"

Dad says, "You have five minutes to find the bathroom and use it, Quinn."

Suddenly, I notice my mother is crying.

"My baby is growing up," she says, sniffing.

"And *out*," says Quinn.

"Go," Dad commands, "or hold it until we get home."

Quinn runs off as Dad says, "Give me those Milky Way bars, Gwen. I'll throw them away for you."

Mom says, "Do I *look* like I was born yesterday?"

Clutching the candy bars, she stomps off and makes a dramatic one-act play out of squishing them and throwing them in the trash.

"You're so right, Mom," I say, when she returns. "I'm on

the verge of a whole new life. A brand-new me. Thank you for caring so deeply."

"Of course I care. You're my baby."

With that, my mother dissolves into tears again. Dad mumbles, "We should have used long-term parking."

I hug both my parents and say a quick good-bye. Quinn isn't back from the bathroom yet, but I'm not going to close this window of opportunity.

"I love you!" I shout as I scurry off, carrying my humongous water bottle. The moment I round the corner, out of sight, I slow down and exhale. My summer adventure has officially begun.

There's a small line in front of the metal detector, and I inch forward, closer and closer to my destiny. After I pass through security, I walk by gates one through ten, pass a Starbucks and Mickey D's. I don't stop until I reach the Cinnabon I've been smelling since I entered the food court.

"Caramel Pecanbon," I say to the clerk, my heart pounding. "Heated, with butter."

Hey, it's vegetarian.

The brand-new me begins tomorrow. Right now, I'm starving.

Seventeen

I hate to admit it, but Mom is right. The thrill of air travel wears away after several squished hours of sitting still. I'm glad I had a little exercise in the parking lot. I'm glad I had a Cinnabon, too, even though it's puffed up in my stomach like an extra airline pillow. The "grilled" chicken dinner they put in front of me tastes like tofu. I might as well be home.

"I used to be able to cross my legs in coach," the older woman next to me says. Her orange lipstick has settled in the cracks above her lip. "It's a disgrace what's happened to the airlines. They're like flying buses now."

I smile, smooth out my airline blanket, and lean my head against the window.

"Are you staying in London?" she asks me.

"No," I say. "I'm flying on to Rome."

"Ah, Rome. I remember when it was the toast of Europe. Now Rome is full of cars and pollution."

I nod, adjust my headphones.

"Did they make you take off your shoes in security?" she asks. "What's next? Body cavity searches?"

What I wouldn't give, at this moment, for a Milky Way Mini.

Nodding again, I snuggle up to the window and pretend to fall asleep. No way am I going to listen to ten and a half hours of griping. Not when I'm on the verge of a brand-new me.

For the rest of the night, I sleep a little, pee twice (thanks, Mom), watch a rerun of *Two and a Half Men*, listen to my iPod, read, pretend to sleep, and stare out the window. I try to watch a movie, but all I can really hear in my headphones is the roar of the engine.

"They used to show movies on a bigger screen," the old lady next to me says the instant my eyes are open, "not these tiny individual screens. It's like watching a movie through a peephole!"

Again, I nod. Then, I shut my eyes and refuse to open them again until I feel sunlight on my face.

In my mind, I play my own movie. *Hayley's Incredible Shrinking Summer.* I envision jogging every morning past Roman ruins, eating nothing but tomato sauce. My heart pinches when I flash on Jackie and Drew. Missing Jackie. Wishing Drew liked me. Cringing at the thought of them together. Proud of my maturity in dealing with the possibility and stepping aside. Actually, Drew and Jackie would make a great couple. She's the girl I've always wanted to be; he's the guy I've always wanted to have. What could be a better fit?

"We're late," the old lady says as my eyelids gently open to the awesome sight of the sun rising above the clouds. I have no idea where I am, but it looks like heaven. Before the black cloud seated next to me can bring me down, I turn my headphones up. My heart thumps. In a few more hours, I'll be landing on a totally foreign chunk of Earth. Everyone I know and love is thousands of miles away. A zap of fear runs through my veins.

"Chill out, Hayley," I say to myself. "You're a big girl." Then I add, chuckling, "*Too* big, but we'll take care of that this summer."

At least the first stop is England. Thank God I don't have to worry about not speaking the language.

"Fancy a bickie or crisps?"

"You lot had best leg it for the loo."

"How naff, you duffer!"

In London's Heathrow Airport, I'm in a parallel universe. I hear my native tongue, but I barely understand a word.

"I'm gobsmacked over those trainers. They're absolutely brill!"

As I follow the signs to my connecting flight, the bustle of London's main airport wakes me up. It's *gorgeous*. Like LAX after finishing school. There are expensive shops, sushi bars, and dark, leathery pubs. Since I'll be landing in Rome at dinnertime—six o'clock—I figure I'd better grab a bite now. Patrice lives far outside of the city. By the time we get to her house, I will have missed dinner altogether.

I check my watch. I have about an hour. How absolutely brill!

"Fish and chips, please," I order, feeling majorly grown-up at a table in one of the pubs. "And a Coke."

My diet doesn't start until I reach Italy. When in England . . .

Grease oozes out of the fried coating of the fish when I take a bite. The chips—really french fries—are salty and hot. My Coke is sweet and cold. This may be the best meal I've had *ever.*

Sadly, the service is slow and I don't have time for dessert. Not if I want to leg it to the loo before I get on the plane to Rome. Raising my hand in the air, I make that squiggly motion I've seen my dad make when he wants the waiter to bring the check. Seems it's an international squiggle, because the waiter instantly nods. I reach into my wallet necklace and freeze. I only have euros! This is England. The one thing I remember from my European History class last year—besides the fact that King Henry VIII "divorced" two of his six wives by cutting off their heads—is that England refused to change their money to euros. Which totally annoys Europeans who like to travel as easily as Americans do.

"I'm so sorry," I say to the waiter when he brings the check. "Is there somewhere I can exchange my euros?"

"Easy peasy," he says.

I stare up at him, my mouth open.

"No problem, luv," he translates. "We take euros."

Whew. I pay, leave an enormous tip, and head for the gate.

England is a whole other universe.

Three hours later, I land in another galaxy.

Eighteen

"Felice di vederti!"

Patrice's husband—I think—flings his arms around me and lifts me off my feet right there in the Rome airport. He squeezes me so hard I'm afraid I might pop. Thanks to Latin class, I recognize the word *felice*. I know he's *happy*. Which, of course, is obvious by his enormous grin and the juicy kisses he plants on both my cheeks.

"Hayley!"

Suddenly, I'm surrounded by the whole *famiglia*.

"I missed your arrival!" Patrice cries, kissing me on both cheeks, too. "Gianna needed to use the *ritirata* and Taddeo's frog got loose."

Frog?

"You met my husband, Gino?"

Gino kisses me again.

Patrice says, "Hayley, you look just like your mother!"

Before I can absorb that blow, Gino hits me with another punch to the gut.

"Che bella faccia!" he says.

Patrice doesn't have to translate. Five thousand miles from home and I'm still the girl with the pretty face. I sigh.

"You're tired," Patrice says. "Let's get you home."

Patrice De Luca looks nothing like my mother. She's rounded and soft. Everything about her is relaxed. Her dyed red hair falls effortlessly to her shoulders. She wears loose white capri pants and a man's shirt. Her brown eyes match her tanned skin. Gino looks like a balloon in the Macy's Thanksgiving parade—all puffed up and proud. His black hair is cropped short and his intense blue eyes are surrounded by deep laugh lines.

"Do you know Britney Spears?" Gianna asks me, tugging on my shirt.

I laugh. About ten years old, Gianna is stick thin, with long straight black hair and eyes that are nearly as dark. Her little brother, Taddeo, is a miniature version of his dad.

"You speak English!" I say to Gianna.

Taddeo replies, "So do me!"

He then reaches into his pocket and produces a tiny, croaking frog.

"Regalo," he says, handing the frog to me. Thankfully,

Patrice guides the frog right back into Taddeo's pocket.

"Give Hayley her gift when we get home," she says.

"What about Ashlee Simpson?" Gianna asks. "Do you know *her*?"

"Britney? Ashlee? Gianna, we've got to talk."

As we make our way to the baggage claim—which they intelligently call baggage *re*claim—I'm in sensory overload. Italians flail their hands while they yell across the grubby airport, beautiful women with bright gold jewelry and sky-high, spiked heels strut across the floor, men with mops of dark hair and butt-hugging suit jackets scoop up luggage. I don't understand a word, but I imagine what everyone is saying.

"Hurry! The parking rates are atrocious!"

"Did you get the Tofurky sandwich I packed for you?"

"Wait! I have to pee!"

Or something like that.

Inside, I'm feeling a mixture of total excitement and utter exhaustion. I can't believe I'm actually here. Plus, it's dawning on me that I don't know these people *at all*. I mean, I knew they were strangers before I left Santa Monica, but seeing them up close and personal underscores it. Another zap of terror shoots through me. Will I be sharing a room with Miss Tweenie Bopper?

"Gianna is the American name for John, only for a girl," Gianna says. "At least that's what my best friend, Romy, says. But she's German even though she lives in Italy. I first learned English in school, but I *really* learned it last summer at camp in England. I'm *so* happy to practice with you! Mom speaks Italian mostly for Dad. He speaks English a little, but not as much as I do. Because of my summer in England. Did I already tell you? My English is perfect, isn't it? That's what my teacher said. Have you ever met Nick Lachey?"

I shake my head no and think, *Oh, God.*

Gianna chatters nonstop as my summer *famiglia* and I snake through the crowd, grab my suitcase off the conveyor belt, and make our way to a car that's so small I half expect a bunch of clowns to jump out of it.

"Taddeo, you sit on my lap," Patrice says.

Gianna and I squeeze into the backseat.

"We go to Assisi!" Gino shouts as he pulls out of the parking lot.

"*Sì, sì!*" Taddeo and Gianna shout back.

No, I'm not in Santa Monica anymore.

The outskirts of Rome Fiumicino Airport could be the outskirts of a big-city airport anywhere. A crowded highway, smog, honking cars with maniac drivers. Somehow, I'd expected to see the Colosseum or the Forum or some other ancient ruin in the distance. Maybe the outline of Vatican City? Instead, I might as well be driving past downtown LA.

"We'll take a trip to Rome later in the summer," Patrice says. "For now, you see the *real* Italy."

After about an hour on the road, I see exactly what she means.

Driving into the countryside of Italy is like traveling back in time. Elderly men ride bicycles along the edge of the road. Old women in rayon dresses and flat black shoes walk to the market. Small mountains rise up in the distance on either side of us. No, I won't be jogging past any Roman ruins. Everything is *green.* The entire landscape is a series of moss-colored lines—rows of grapevines, olive trees, and tall, skinny cypresses. Lush vegetable gardens sprout in every front yard. And the flowers! Red poppies dot the green fields, pink blossoms burst out from window boxes, curbs explode in yellow blooms.

"It's gorgeous," I say, dead tired, yet totally awake.

"Umbria is the most beautiful region in Italy," Patrice says. "But I'm biased."

We drive past Narni and Terni and a bunch of villages whose names end in vowels. Almost all the houses are made out of stone. It's as if they've grown directly out of the earth.

Even though it's nearly eight o'clock in the evening, it's light and warm. We're jammed in the tiny car with all the windows open and no air-conditioning. Yet, somehow, I'm not sweating. The air smells sweet. And it seems to glow all around me in a faint orange color.

"Desidera cena?" Gino asks me, as if I can understand him.

"We hope you're hungry," Patrice explains. "We have an

Umbrian feast waiting for you at home."

"It's so late," I protest.

Patrice laughs. "Italians always eat dinner this late. Or later."

I swallow. Then I make some quick calculations in my mind. Technically, my body is still on U.S. time. I don't have to start my diet until tomorrow when I *wake up* in Italy.

"I'm starved," I say.

When in the outskirts of Rome . . .

Nineteen

I see by the signs that Assisi is near. But I'm completely unprepared for the sight that fills my eyes. Gino drives over a ridge, under two trees whose leaves have joined on top to form a tunnel, and there it is.

"Wow!" I gasp.

Rising up—a glowing orange stone fortress—is the old town of Assisi. It's literally built *into* the green mountain, like an intricate sand castle on the side of a hill. Or a golden wedding cake reaching far into the sky. The tower at the top seems like it's miles in the air.

"You live up there?" I ask, agog.

"No," Gino says. "We live *qui*."

With that, he makes a sharp right turn onto a dirt road

and drives up to a black wrought-iron gate. Patrice points a tiny remote control at the entrance, and the gate slowly opens. After Gino drives through, the gate closes behind us. Inside, the car rumbles along a narrow road shadowed by overhanging trees. Then, the landscape opens up and I gasp again.

"That's your house?" I ask. "It looks like a castle."

Patrice laughs. Gianna claps her hands.

There's no turret, but the "castle" is the most beautiful home I've ever seen. Three stories high, it's made completely of stone—the color of pink sand. The roof is tiled with overlapping terra cotta. Chocolate brown shutters flank every window. A large green vine grows up the front and spans the entire house.

Gino stops the car before he reaches the house.

"And you live *qui*," he says to me.

Across the road from the big main house is a tall stone cottage.

"What do you mean?" I ask.

Patrice says, "We call it La Torre, the tower, because it's narrow and high and looks out over Assisi."

"I get to stay *there*?" I ask, nearly losing my breath.

"Every sixteen-year-old needs a bit of privacy, no?"

I am *definitely* not in Santa Monica anymore!

I can't believe my eyes—or my luck. La Torre is *awesome*. A smaller, older version of the main house. Ancient russet-colored rectangular stones rise up two floors. The mortar between them is a thin line of gray. A giant red rosebush grows higher than the front door. And around the side, an outdoor spiral staircase leads up to the second floor.

"Your bedroom and bathroom are upstairs," Patrice says, as we unfold ourselves out of the car. "A living room and kitchen are downstairs, though we hope you'll want to eat with us."

"Of course," I say, unable to close my gaping mouth.

"Take a moment to get settled. We'll have supper outside."

While Patrice and Gianna prepare dinner, Gino lugs my suitcase up the narrow spiral staircase. Holding my hand, Taddeo shows me the downstairs.

"For cold," he says, pointing to a small refrigerator. Indicating a tiny stove, he adds, "For hot."

Even though it's still warm outside, it's cool in the tower. The floors, walls, and ceilings are all stone. The kitchen sink is a large marble basin. There's a little table and chairs beneath one of the two windows, and a small couch sits in front of an old fireplace set into the far wall. I *love* it.

Suddenly looking shy, Taddeo reaches into his pocket and gently retrieves the frog.

"For you," he says, holding Mr. Ribbit in the air.

I'm touched. And totally grossed out.

"How sweet, Taddeo!" I say, jamming both hands into the front pockets of my snug jeans. No easy feat, but no way am I taking that slimy thing.

"Can you take care of it for me?" I ask. "At your house?"

He agrees, and the poor frog goes back in his pocket.

"Come." Taddeo tugs my elbow and I follow him outside. Around the corner, we climb the spiral staircase—each step echoing on the metal treads. At the top, I pause for a moment to look out over the beautiful land. I've never seen so many shades of green.

Taddeo pushes through the thick wood door and leads me into the bedroom of my dreams.

"For sleep," he says, pointing to the huge, king-sized bed.

An ornate metal headboard anchors the bed to one wall. My suitcase sits on top of a beautiful yellow bedspread, with big red flowers—the same fabric as the drapes. Gino heads out, opening both large windows. Through one, I see gorgeous Assisi in the distance. Through the other, a large oak tree with a swing hanging from it. It feels like we're all alone in paradise. No neighbors are visible. Nothing but the sounds of birds.

Overhead is a high, stone ceiling, supported by thick timber beams. Underfoot, the same stone floor as downstairs. Both have a pinkish hue. Both are stunning.

"E qui," Taddeo says, completing the tour, "for private."

He opens a small wooden door and steps back. I enter the bathroom, which is perfect for one. There's a small sink and shower, plus a toilet. No scale, I notice, talking or otherwise. The walls are tiled in white, with two fluffy cherry-red towels hanging on the back of the door.

"It's beautiful," I say to Taddeo.

"*La cena!*" Gino shouts from outside.

Taddeo runs out, and I follow him down the stairs to my first Italian feast.

On a shady patch of green lawn between the castle and the tower, a long wooden table is *covered* in food. Before I can stop her, Patrice puts a little of everything on my plate.

"Tonight we taste Umbria," she says.

"*Salame e* truffles *da* Norcia, *prosciutto di* Parma, olive oil *da* Foligno, *strangozzi* pasta *con* pesto *d'*Assisi." With each serving, Gino proudly announces its nearby origin. My mouth waters. No tofu in sight. And meat, glorious meat!

"*Vino rosso d'* Orvieto, *Parmigiano-Regg*—"

"Red wine?" I say, holding the glass he's poured for me. "I'm sixteen."

He looks confused. Patrice says, "Italians drink red wine at any age. And almost every meal," she adds, laughing.

"Ah," Gino says, catching on. "*Vino rosso è sangue.*"

"Blood?" I ask. Thank you again, Latin class!

"*Sì, sì,*" Gino says. "Red wine is Italian blood. Americans drink alcohol to get drunk. Italians drink wine to be alive."

He raises his class and says, "*Alla salute!*"

"*Saluti,*" I repeat. To your health. I take a sip. The only other alcoholic beverage I've tried before is beer, and I hated it. Beer, to me, tastes like soda gone bad. I assumed wine would taste the same. But it's totally different. A bit bitter, the red wine tastes like the earth. It's fruity and smoky and sweet and sour all at once. I'm not crazy about it, but it's interesting.

"Wine in the U.S. has more alcohol in it than it does here," Patrice explains. "You can drink wine in Italy without getting drunk."

I take another sip.

As the sun slowly fades, the backdrop of old Assisi begins to shine with the city's nighttime lights. As I watch it up on the hill, I see the color change from light orange to pink to gold. It's truly an awesome sight.

"Rendiamo grazie a dio," Gino begins, bowing his head and linking hands with me and Gianna. The rest of the family holds hands across the table. *"Per nostra amica americana e per questo pasto. Amen."*

Did he just thank God for me and pasta?

"Amen," everyone murmurs.

"Mangia!"

The feast begins. My heart is thudding. It all looks and smells so scrumptious I don't know where to start. My first bite is the pasta with pesto. The pasta is chewy and slightly sweet, the pesto tastes garlicky and green. My tastebuds explode with joy. Silently, I, too, thank God for pasta . . . and for everything else. With each bite, I have a new experience. The salami is smoky and dry, the cheese is nutty. And the truffles—sort of like earthy mushrooms—are grated over flatbread brushed with sweet olive oil. They taste woodsy and rich and indescribably delicious.

My stomach sinks.

I'm never going to make it.

Ten weeks of food this good?

In a panic, I gobble everything up quickly, my head bent over the plate. When I come up for air, the entire family is staring at me.

"Yum," I say guiltily.

Gino reaches his hand over to my hand and gently pushes my fork down to the table. "Food is like falling in love," he says. "You cannot rush either one."

Okay, so I'm Porky Pig. Can you blame me? I've never tasted food that is actually made in the vicinity. The only thing manufactured in Santa Monica is almost everyone's *nose*.

"What is your house like in America?" Gianna asks.

"It's an apartment," I answer.

"Do Americans like Italians?"

"Yes."

"Do you drive a big car?"

"No."

"Are American girls as mean as they seem in books?"

I laugh. "You're reading the wrong books."

"Who is your fav—"

"Gianna, let Hayley eat in peace," Patrice says.

Gianna pouts, but doesn't argue. For the rest of the

meal, in a mixture of Italian, English, and Latin, I find out about my new summer family. Gino works for some government council in Perugia, about twenty kilometers away. However far *that* is. The stone castle and tower have been in his family for generations. Patrice and my mom were roommates at UCLA, until Patrice left for Italy to study art. She met Gino in a tiny Perugian trattoria.

"He was eating pasta with truffles, I was eating an artichoke salad," Patrice says. "We were both alone, so we shared our meal, our wine, and ultimately, our lives."

Gino steps up from the table and kisses his wife on the lips.

"Amore mio," he says.

I sigh. If Drew Wyler ever said, "My love," to me that way, I'd melt into a puddle of pesto right there on the spot.

It seems like hours before everyone is finished eating. And I marvel at how odd it is not to be watching *Wheel of Fortune*. I can't remember a dinner at home without my dad yelling, "Buy a vowel!" and Mom musing over Vanna White's hair ("She's curly today!").

"Baci?" Patrice asks at the end of dinner, handing me Italy's version of the Hershey's kiss.

"Are you sure you're friends with my mom?" I ask, smiling and taking one. All I can say is that the Italian chocolate kisses are so delicious I could have an entire make-out session with them. If eating is falling in love, I just met the meal I plan to marry.

I can't wait to tell Jackie all about my first night. Though the time difference is insane—when it's ten at night in Italy, it's one in the afternoon in California—I know she's waiting to hear from me.

"Could I please use your computer tonight?" I ask Patrice, rising to help her clear the dishes.

"I don't have a computer, honey," she says.

The warm air suddenly goes still. "Does Gino?"

"No."

"Gianna?"

"The kids are allowed to use computers at school. But at home, I want them to read books and relate to us instead of staring at a computer screen."

I can't help but notice that Gianna is getting her American popular culture from somewhere. Not that I'd ever call Britney, Ashlee, or Nick cultured.

Mom warned me not to use the De Lucas' phone, unless I was dialing *her* number and reversing the charges. Calling California from Italy is ridiculously expensive. It never occurred to us that there would be no Internet access. At least not to *me*. Is this my mother's evil plan to get me to read more?

"Does your phone text?" I ask Patrice.

"Nope. It's doesn't do laundry, either."

I chuckle weakly. "So, how do you . . . communicate?"

Patrice laughs. "The mailman comes regularly."

Mailman?

"Italy operates at a leisurely pace, Hayley. You'll feel much happier if you accept it."

Leisurely pace? I know their houses are made of stone, but who imagined they were in the Stone *Age*? I'm supposed to talk to Jackie through the mail? What's next? A horse and buggy? What have I gotten myself into?

After helping with the dishes and calling my parents (collect!) to let them know I'd arrived safely, I say good night to the De Lucas and climb the outdoor staircase to my bedroom. Laying flat on the bed, I stare up at the beamed ceiling and try to imagine using a stamp instead of a send button.

"Ughhh." I groan out loud. I'm never going to make it.

My distended stomach rises like a loaf of crusty Italian bread. The salty tang of prosciutto is still on my tongue. Garlic is on my breath. Rolling out of bed, I slap my bare feet across the stone floor and enter the bathroom.

"Hayley," I say sternly to my reflection in the mirror, "tomorrow is a new beginning. Embrace the experience. Look forward, not behind."

Reaching around to feel the width of my ass, I add, "Good God, never look at your behind."

My plan is simple. Tomorrow morning, after I make my mother proud by insisting on doing the breakfast dishes—even though I will only have a cup of black coffee and a small piece of fruit—I'll jog up the hill to Assisi and find an Internet café. The whole country can't be disconnected, can it? After I e-mail Jackie, I'll explore my new town. I'll scope it out for cute boys, nice girls, anyone who speaks English. I'll eat only vegetables, drink gallons of water, and walk briskly, rolling my foot from heel to toe. My journey to the brand-new me will begin at sunrise.

Before turning out the light, I catch my reflection once more.

"*Ciao*, old Hayley," I say. "Tomorrow, meet the new you."

Twenty

The new me sleeps until eleven.

"I'm so sorry," I say, running into Patrice's kitchen. She's at the sink, rinsing off the biggest, roundest, reddest tomatoes I've ever seen.

"For what?" she asks.

"I guess I'll need an alarm clock," I say sheepishly.

"Alarm clock? In the summer? What's wrong with the one God gave you?"

"Huh?" I ask.

Patrice dries her hands and walks over to me.

"Do you know why you're here, Hayley?" she asks.

I almost answer, "To lose weight," but I suspect she's fishing for the deeper reason.

"To experience a different way of life?" I offer.

"Exactly. Now, stop trying to control it, and start *feeling* it."

She sounds just like my English teacher, Ms. Antonucci. I'm not sure how to go about *feeling* Italy, unless, of course, I count the sensation of fat cells building a stone farmhouse on each thigh. I can still taste the garlic from dinner. And last night I dreamed my name was changed to Hayley *Salami*. Sounds a bit Middle Eastern, but tastes amazing.

"Sit. Eat." A plate full of almond biscotti and a glass of orange juice is waiting for me at the table.

I say, "Just coffee and fru—"

Patrice scoffs. "Don't be ridiculous. Breakfast is the most important meal of the day . . . even if you eat it in the afternoon!"

"Are you *sure* you know my mother?" I ask, laughing.

She answers, "Italy changes your whole perspective. You'll see."

With that, she pours me a large glass of milk. Incredibly, I'm starving. The cold milk slithers down my throat. The biscotti are crunchy and nutty and delicious. The orange juice is freshly squeezed and perfectly tart.

I stifle a groan.

The first day of the brand-new me and I've already failed.

"Fruit and cheese?" Patrice asks, standing at the open refrigerator.

The De Luca kitchen is exactly how I imagined an Italian countryside kitchen to look. A large rectangular antique table is the centerpiece. A painted ceramic bowl filled with lemons and limes sits on it, sending a citrus aroma through the air. Sunlight floods the room. Fresh herbs grow in a window box behind the huge farm sink. White marble countertops meet old salmon-colored tiles that rise up a foot against the stone walls. The floor and walls are the same pinkish hue that's in my tower. Next to the huge stainless steel stove—the only modern thing in the room besides the refrigerator and dishwasher—is a large cooking fireplace. About waist high, the charred logs sit under an oven rack. The faint smell of roasted meat is still in the air.

"Your kitchen is awesome," I say.

"It's the heart and soul of our home," she replies.

I flash on our kitchen in Santa Monica. It's more like the dungeon. Tiny and dark, it's the room my whole family avoids. Mom and I, because temptation lives there. Dad and Quinn, because tofu lives there. I cringe to think of how many times I'd preferred to sit in my car, in the parking lot of a drive-thru, than go home for dinner.

The rest of the De Luca home is an emotional reflection of the kitchen—comfortable, welcoming, warm, and old. You can feel the spirits of the De Lucas who've lived here before.

"Where is everybody?" I ask Patrice as I finish breakfast—

including a *small* piece of Parmesan cheese with the best peach I've ever tasted.

"Gino is at work, and the kids are outside enjoying their lives. Which, *cara mia*," she says, wrapping her fleshy arms around me, "is precisely what I want you to do. But first, the house *regole*."

"Rules?"

"*Sì*. Number One: Unless we know where you are, you must be home while you can still read outside. That's how we define darkness here. Number Two: If you're going to miss lunch or dinner, let me know because I will always set a place for you. Number Three: There's a bicycle around the back of the house that you can use all summer, but I don't want you driving the car. Italian drivers are certifiable. And, Number Four: This is *your* summer, not mine to create for you. You're completely safe to explore on your own, or ask me if you want to take a day trip somewhere. I've left a few books about Umbria for you in the tower. I'll happily take you anywhere you want to go, but it has to be at *your* request, okay?"

I nod. Without warning, my eyes tear up.

"I haven't said 'Thank you' yet, have I?"

Patrice hands me my own remote to open the front gate, and a piece of paper with her phone number on it.

"We are incredibly happy to have you here," she says, hugging me. "Now go."

|||||||||||||||||||||

The sun is high and lemon yellow. It's way too hot to jog, but I'm flexible. Dressed in flip-flops, khaki Bermuda shorts, and a white T-shirt, I set out to feel my new life by walking briskly up the hill to Assisi and e-mailing Jackie. Instantly, I wish I'd worn my hair up.

"It's okay," I say out loud to myself. "*Feel* the sweat."

The road leading up to Assisi is a two-lane street without sidewalks. Patrice wasn't kidding when she said Italian drivers are certifiable. Several pass me so fast it looks like they're in the final lap of the Indy 500. And clearly, they consider lane markers only as a suggestion. So each time I hear a car coming, I leap into the tall grass beside the road. Why experience being splatted on someone's windshield?

Old Assisi looms large up ahead. The closer I get, the more beautiful it looks. The whole city is the same color— a pinkish orange in the bright sunlight. On the way, I pass a green field full of horses, a private home with its own rose garden, and a hotel that looks like the De Lucas' stone house. As I walk, the incline grows steeper. My sweaty feet slide forward in my flip-flops. My thighs rub the fabric of my shorts together. My heavy hair sticks to the back of my neck.

By the time I reach the base of the town, huffing and puffing, I'm red-faced and dripping sweat. Italy? In *summer*? What was I thinking? Why would I start liking heat just because people speak Italian in it?

There's a big parking lot at the bottom of the even bigger

hill of Assisi. Several souvenir stands line one edge of it. Thankfully, one of them sells bottles of cold water.

"*Gelato?*" the woman behind the counter asks me. She points to a freezer full of luscious ice cream. *Be strong,* I tell myself.

"No, *grazie,*" I say. "Just water."

With the cold bottle of water in my hand, I find a shady spot and sit down. I wait for a breeze, but it doesn't come. So I just sit there, sipping my water, telling myself not to (literally!) sweat it—I have all day to explore, all summer to lose thirty pounds, all my life to learn how to love sunshine.

Finally, my shirt has dried and I'm ready to renew my trek up the hill. With the first step, however, I'm in trouble. My flip-flop straps have created two huge blisters between my first and second toes. No way can I walk without hobbling.

"*Memorize every moment.*" I hear Ms. Antonucci's voice in my head and I laugh. Moment One: Yeowww!

"There's only one thing to do," I say to myself. "Hobble into town and buy new shoes."

Off I go, slapping my feet ahead of me in an attempt to keep the offending flip-flops away from the blisters. How hard can it be to find a shop that sells cheap shoes?

I pass another hotel, totter under an ancient archway, and gasp. Assisi is *gorgeous.* Everything is stone. Even the street. Yellow and purple flowers bloom on terraces all the way up the hill. It looks like a jeweled staircase. Several small store windows display religious artifacts from Saint Francis, the saint who was born in Assisi. Others show beautiful painted dishes in gold and blue. Still others have mounds of pastries sitting enticingly on glass shelves. Up ahead, thank God, I see a shoe store. Wincing, I scurry over, reach for the door, and stop. It's locked.

Closed? I glance at my watch. How could a shoe store be closed on a weekday at one o'clock? Then I take a second look around. *Every* store is closed. In fact, I suddenly notice there's hardly anyone outside at all.

"Excuse me." I stop the first woman who walks by. She looks cosmopolitan. Her toenails are painted bright red.

"I'm so sorry, I don't speak Italian," I say. "Do you speak any English?"

"Yes," she answers. "Can I help you?"

"Is this some kind of Italian holiday or something?"

"No. Why do you ask?"

"The stores are all closed."

She bursts out laughing. "This is your first time to Italy, no?"

"*Sì,*" I say.

"Everything closes in the afternoon for *riposo.*"

"The whole city closes for a nap?" I ask, agog.

"We eat, we drink wine, we sleep. Sometimes we make love," she says, smiling. "If the weather is not too hot."

Wiping my sweaty forehead, I say, "Is it ever not too hot?"

She winks. "I have three children."

We both laugh. She tells me that the Italian lunch "hour" is from one to three. Most stores open again by four or five.

"Lunch?" I stop suddenly.

"In Italy, the whole *famiglia* gathers together for lunch. It's part of our culture."

"Grazie," I shout, hobbling quickly down the hill.

"Prego," she calls after me.

My very first day, and I've already violated *regola* Number Two! Even though I just ate breakfast, I'm about to miss lunch without telling Patrice. Quickly, I look around for a phone booth. There is none in sight. I guess a modern phone booth in this beautiful medieval town would be like a zit on Scarlett Johansson's cheek.

I take my flip-flops off and, my feet burning on the hot road, run back down the hill until I can run no more.

Twenty-One

"Hayley!" Gino calls to me from the outdoor table, though his accent drops the "H" and it sounds like "Ayley."

"I'm *so* sorry," I say, my chest heaving. "I totally spaced on the time."

Patrice laughs. "I didn't expect you for lunch *today*, Hayley. You just ate breakfast."

"Sit. Eat." Gino flags me over. Gianna moves down one chair to make room for me.

"No, *grazie*," I say. "I couldn—is that pizza?"

"American pizza is cheese and . . ." He turns to Patrice and asks, *"Come si dice cartone?"*

Gianna squeals, "Cardboard!"

"Sì, sì. American pizza is cheese and cardboard. Taste the real thing."

I sit, cool my sore, bare feet in the soft grass beneath the table, and bite into a piece of grilled flatbread with juicy sun-dried tomatoes, fresh sprigs of basil, and gently melted mozzarella cheese. The different flavors spread through my mouth, exciting my tongue. The real thing is *amazing*. Gino hands me a glass of red wine. Taddeo hands me a rock he found that morning. Gianna asks, "Do you have an American boyfriend?"

I smile. I'm home.

Up in my bedroom after lunch, it's surprisingly cool. Even without air-conditioning, the stone walls keep the heat out. The open window beneath the shade of the old oak tree lets a soft breeze seep through. A hawk's insistent cry pierces the silence. The dishes are done, the food is put away, and the whole *famiglia* is either asleep or making love.

I could get used to this life.

Flipping through the book on Umbria that Patrice bought for me, I uncover interesting facts about my summer home. Umbria is the most hilly region of Italy. Saint Francis—the guy who was born in Assisi—was once a rich kid who spurned his family's dough and lived in poverty and prayer. Other guys were so impressed, they followed his lead and gave up all their stuff to become "Franciscan" monks, who wore only brown robes and sandals. Saint Francis also had some Doctor Dolittle action going on. Everywhere he went, animals flocked around him.

It's hard to decide exactly what I want to see this summer. Umbria is full of medieval hill towns and luscious countryside. Not to mention awesome churches and ancient piazzas. And of course, there's Rome. Which, I discover, is technically in the region next door. Still, I'd love to see the Sistine Chapel and statues of all those hot Roman bods. Plus, as I read in the book, Romans love a type of Italian bacon called *pancetta.*

"Hayley?" There's a soft knock on my door.

"Come on in," I say, standing.

Patrice steps through the door. "I thought you might be asleep."

I laugh. "I just woke up three hours ago."

Smiling, Patrice says, "This country has a way of lulling you into slumber. But I'm glad you're awake. I want to show you something."

We sit side by side on the bed—which is neatly tucked thanks to the promise I made my mom. Patrice flips open a photo album.

"Recognize her?" she asks me.

A face like my own beams at the camera. A woman is leaping into shallow waves at the beach. She wears one of those flowered bikinis that is tied at each hip. Her stomach is flat; her thighs long and lean.

"Mom?" I say, flabbergasted.

"Hard to believe we were ever that young," says Patrice.

I stare at the photo. Though I've seen shots of my

younger mom before, they've always been pictures of Thanksgiving dinners and robed graduations and photos of her cradling me or Quinn. Each one plumper than the previous. This is the first time I've seen my mother's flat bare stomach.

"We were pretty wild back then," Patrice says.

Patrice turns the page. Still in her bikini, Mom is riding piggyback, her bare legs encircling some cute guy's torso. (Definitely *not* my dad.) On another page, there's a photo of my mother dancing—her big hair a mass of permed curls. In another shot, she's playfully nibbling some guy's earlobe. I can barely believe my eyes. She looks so . . . different. So *relaxed*. The number of Waist Watcher units in a Peep seems the farthest thing from her mind.

"I can't believe I've never seen these photos before," I say.

Patrice runs her hand down the back of my hair. "Your mother gave them all to me."

"Why?"

She inhales deeply. "Sometimes it's hard to face who you once were."

I flip the page and see a bright afternoon shot of Mom and Patrice strolling though the UCLA campus. Both faces tilted toward the sun.

"Is it hard for you?" I ask.

Patrice sighs. "Let's just say it's a lifelong struggle to keep that girl's spirit alive."

All at once, I get it. I realize what my mom—the Tofu

Queen—wants for me. Before it's too late, she wants her daughter to feel what she once felt: invincible. A girl's spirit. Not the keeper of a secret inner self. Not a girl who hates the beach and camis and Abercrombie and Fitch. Mom wants me to feel *free*. The way she felt so long ago. Of course, buying me a trash-talking scale is *so* not the way to go about it. Still, I suddenly see where her heart lies. Even in candid shots around campus, with Mom wearing an off-the-shoulder sweatshirt and stonewashed jeans, it's clear that my mother feels *whole*. Her body is connected to her soul. She's a person. Not a big butt, or ham thighs, or arms without definition. She's just . . . *her*. The way she wants her daughter to feel.

Just me.

"Thank you," I say softly.

Patrice smiles and gets up to go, leaving the photo album behind.

"You'll be here for dinner?" she asks.

"Wouldn't miss it," I reply.

As I hear her footsteps descend the spiral staircase, I lie back on the bed, the photo album resting on my chest. I let my eyes fall closed. In a matter of seconds, I'm dead asleep. Dreaming, this time, of flying.

Twenty-Two

Day One was a wash. Or a total joy. Depending on whether you look at it as an American or an Italian. I decide to be Italian. Why stress over a day spent eating and sleeping and looking at a photo album?

Today, my spirit is revived. Not quite free enough to romp around in a bikini, but definitely ready to stride up the hill to Assisi. But I've wised up. I'm now wearing sneakers with double sockettes. My hair is knotted high on my head. I'm borrowing the bike, and on the road by ten in the morning.

Assisi still looms large ahead of me. I've decided to take it slow. Travel the Italian way. If I'm not pulverized by a speeding Fiat, I'll get there in plenty of time to find an

Internet café, e-mail Jackie and my parents, and make it home by lunch.

"Buon giorno!" I shout to everyone I pass.

"Ciao!" they shout back, which must mean both *hi* and *bye* in the same way *aloha* does.

It's a glorious morning. The sun is amber and the scenery is bright green. My thighs ache as I pedal up the hill, but I'm enjoying the sensation. It's been a long time since I had any feeling in there. It's nice to feel my muscles wake up after such a long *riposo*. By the time I reach the base of old Assisi, I'm ready to park and lock my bike, buy a bottle of water, and go straight to the top.

It's hard to imagine a city more beautiful than Assisi. Within the old town itself, the cobblestone streets are swept clean and flowers sprout everywhere. As I walk up the steep hill, I pass fountains, shrines to Saint Francis, small trattorias on large terraces with umbrella-covered tables and glistening bottles of green olive oil. The stores are tiny. There's a butcher, a baker, a soap maker. The lovely smells of life are all around me. Baking bread, lavender, and, of course, garlic. It's all so picturesque, I nearly forget what I'm looking for.

"Excuse me," I say to a man sweeping the stone steps leading into his souvenir shop. *"Parla inglese?"*

"No," he says. Then he proceeds to explain something to me in Italian. Something about his son at the University in Perugia, I think. I just nod and wait for him to finish.

"Internet café?" I ask, when his lips stop moving.

He stares blankly.

Mimicking a keyboard, I type in the air and say, *"Interneto."*

His eyes light up and he nods furiously. Pointing up the hill, he lets me know that I'll see it if I keep walking. Up, of course.

"Grazie," I say. And up I go.

Today, since it's still early, I'm not the only person walking uphill. In fact, there are lots of people on the street. Some tourists, some locals, and an obvious difference between the two. Tourists wear sneakers, shorts, and fanny packs, and carry bottles of water. Locals wear shoes and sandals, dresses, and studded handbags, and never eat or drink *anything* unless they're sitting with family or friends. In fact, one of the most surprising things about Italy so far is the utter lack of fast food. The sight of a Wendy's or a KFC in Assisi would be shocking.

I join bleached-blond tourists and dark-haired Italians walking up in the same direction. Must be aiming for the main piazza. The Umbria book says that every Italian town has one. Which is so cool. We have a mall, they have a town square. If I see a Gap, I'll die.

It's hot, of course, but I decide to ignore it. What better way to lose water weight? Like everyone else, I continue marching up, looking in store windows along the way. Until my gaze locks on something much more enticing. Ahead, three Italian boys my age stand in the shade of an archway over one of the narrow side streets. They look alike. All three have tanned skin and shaggy black hair. They wear skinny shorts down to the knee, high-top sneakers, and thin sweater vests (in the heat!) over untucked white shirts. As I pass by, one of the boys shouts, *"Americana?"*

Instantly, I suck in my gut.

"Sì," I call over my shoulder.

"Statue of Liberty, Monica Lewinsky, Big Mac," he yells.

I nod, then shake my head. He's probably never been to the United States, yet he's able to sum up the best and worst of my country in one sentence. I continue walking up the hill, incredibly glad I'm not wearing a fanny pack, in case he's summing up my ass as well.

I glance back. He is. He grins and I notice a gap between his two front teeth. I also notice eyes that are so blue they're nearly turquoise. *Dangerous eyes,* I say to myself. Those eyes could undress you, lay you down, and rev you up before you had time to blink.

He winks. It would be incredibly smarmy if an American boy winked at me, but this boy—with his smooth brown cheeks—quickens my pulse.

"Ciao," I shout seductively. Then I walk briskly up the hill, cursing my doofy tourist sneakers.

Soon, most of my fellow walkers veer to the left. I follow and continue up a narrow stone sidewalk until I see a sight that takes my breath away. The road expands into a large stone plaza, framed by two long rows of sand-colored arches and columns. At the apex, where the arches meet, an enormous gray fortress rises into the blue sky.

"Piazza?" I ask a passerby.

"Basilica di Santo Francesco" is the reply.

I don't need a phrase book to translate. Ahead of me, looming like a peaceful giant, is the church of Saint Francis. The Internet can wait. This I've got to see.

Passing under the largest of the stone archways, I enter the church through thick dark wood doors. Instantly, I'm struck by the gorgeous bright-blue ceiling. Sky-high, it's painted between crisscrossing curved beams. Enormous stained glass windows let the morning sunlight illuminate wall paintings that cover the entire church.

"So much survived the earthquake," I overhear one tourist tell another.

"Earthquake?" I ask, interrupting.

Turning to me, she asks, "American?"

I hold my breath and nod, hoping she's not going to blame me for every mistake my country has ever made.

"I'm Peggy and this is Bridget," she says, holding out her hand. "We're from Scotland. Edinburgh."

We shake hands as I exhale. Their grins let me know I'm safe.

"Nice to meet you," I say. "I'm Hayley. From California."

Bridget says, "You know all about earthquakes, then."

"Enough to know you don't want to be in one."

"Assisi had a five-point-five in 1997," Peggy explains. "Chunks of these priceless frescoes fell off the walls."

"Oh, no," I groan.

"They were able to save a lot of them. The restoration has been going on ever since."

Each brightly colored panel on the walls depicts a different scene from Saint Francis's life, including the major moment when he cast aside all his worldly possessions. Some spots are blank, but most of the paintings are intact. What a tragedy if this incredible art had been lost.

"Have you seen the tomb?" Peggy asks me.

"Tomb?"

"Saint Francis is buried in the lower basilica. Definitely worth a look. You won't see more beautiful frescoes anywhere."

A monk walks by us in a long brown robe and sandals. The two Scottish women, wearing oversize T-shirts tucked into their oversize shorts, say good-bye as I walk deeper into the Middle Ages. Through the vibrant art on the walls, I learn about Saint Francis—a man who devoted his life to helping the needy. We have Angelina and Brad; the Italians had him.

Almost two hours after I went in, I emerge from both the upper and lower basilicas, awash in art and awe. Unbelievably, the brown tunic worn by Saint Francis is on display in the basement. More than eight hundred years old, I can't help but wonder if his DNA is still on it. I imagine how his saintly clone would view California. Would he toss up his hands at all the Hummers in Los Angeles and condemn the wasteful to hell? Or would he convince the mega-rich of Malibu to open their trophy houses to the homeless? I can see it now—thousands of Southern Californians exchanging Prada for sack cloth.

Outside in the warm sun, I smile as I picture Paris Hilton in a brown robe and flat sandals. With a gold Chanel chain belt, of course.

"The Hill of Hell." Bridget and Peggy are suddenly standing beside me.

"You're not kidding," I say, rubbing the fronts of my sore thighs.

They chuckle. Peggy points to a grassy hill up ahead and says, "It's called the Hill of Hell because public executions were held here in the Middle Ages."

"Ew," I say.

"Which is why Saint Francis chose to be buried here. So he could rest with all the outcasts."

"Not to mention the view," Bridget adds, looking out over the green fields of Umbria. From this height—not even halfway up Assisi—you can see forever. Stone houses dot the landscape like paint strokes of brown and rust. The large dome of another church rises in the distance.

"It's easy to see why some of the greatest artists in the

world are Italian," she says. "Look what they have for inspiration."

I have to agree. California has its beaches and the mansions of Beverly Hills, but it's nothing like looking out over a landscape that's thousands of years old. In Los Angeles, everything old is ugly. In Italy, everything old is art.

"Enjoy the day," Peggy says. Then they both continue the trek upward. I stand still for a moment, on a hill that once held so much sorrow. Incredibly, for the first time in forever, I feel completely and totally *happy*.

"Must be something I ate," I say to myself. Grinning, I turn around and make my way home for lunch.

Twenty-Three

It doesn't take long to settle into an Italian routine. Each day begins and ends the same way. I wake up, inhale the earthy scent of olive trees and new grass, shower, dress, walk down the outdoor spiral staircase, stroll across the lawn to the big house, visit with Patrice and the kids, eat biscotti, drink espresso, and either walk or bike into town. At night, after a late supper with the family, I help with the dishes, play cards with Gianna, then return to my room in the tower to listen to my music or read. The hawk outside my window cries every night. And each night, I'm dumbstruck by how different my life has become. Mostly, in what I *haven't* had for days.

Television.

Fast food.

A cell phone.

A car.

A best friend.

With the exception of missing Jackie, I can't honestly say I long for anything else. And, to my utter astonishment—though my plan to eat less than a thousand calories a day disintegrated after my first bite of Patrice's linguine with garlic and truffle oil—my shorts, shirts, and jeans are getting *looser* every day. I don't need a new wardrobe yet, but the feeling of air between my skin and my clothes is unbelievably delicious.

"You're alive!" Jackie IMs me.

Finally, I find the Internet café on a small street off of Assisi's town square: Piazza del Comune. About midway up the mountain, the square opens like the warm embrace of an Italian nana. Stone (of course!), a circular fountain at one end, trattoria tables at the other, and arched windows in the buildings all around. Mothers with babies lick gelatos in the shade, lovers nuzzle each other's necks as they sit on the edge of the high fountain. Lots of people are in motion, but no one seems to be in a hurry. Especially the Franciscan monks who stroll through the piazza in their long brown robes.

"You're awake!" I type. It's about ten in the morning Italian time, which means it's about one in the morning in Santa Monica.

Jackie writes, "Can't sleep. Too lonely."

I smile. No way can I tell her I've been crashing every afternoon after lunch.

"No computer," I type.

"No *way*!" Jackie replies.

"It's OK," I write, surprised that it actually is. "I'm in an Internet café sipping espresso."

"GRN w NV!"

Instantly, my mind flashes on Drew Wyler.

"Wuz new?" I ask, holding my breath.

"Night surfing sucks," she replies.

I laugh. "Doing anything else interesting at night?"

"Does a pedicure count as interesting?" she types.

"God, I hope not," I type back.

"Then, no. Zip."

In spite of myself, I exhale, relieved. Not that I want Jackie to have a bad summer. Honestly. It's just that my head is way ahead of my heart when it comes to imagining my best friend and my never-to-be-boyfriend together.

"Italy is awesome," I type.

"Wish I was there," she types back.

"Wish you were here, too."

"*Ciao, mia amica,*" Jackie writes.

"Your Italian is better than mine!"

"I looked it up."

"LOL."

"Luv U."

"U 2."

Revved by my espresso and chat with Jackie, I quickly send my parents an e-mail ("Assisi is awesome! Luv U!"), then I step back out in the Italian sun. Today, my goal is the Chiesa Nuova, another old church farther up the hill. Supposedly, this church was built on the site where Saint Francis's family once lived. Which gives you an inkling of how tight their butts must have been in those days. Climbing this high just to come home? Even though Francis's family had serious bling, I doubt that they had delivery. I can just imagine his mom screeching, "You forgot the milk! How many times do I have to remind you?" Or maybe they had their own cow just outside the back door.

Each day, my goal is to get higher up the steep hill of Assisi until I reach the top: Rocca Maggiore, which I've been calling "Major Rock" even though Patrice told me it means *large fortress*. It's a medieval military fort with an awesome view of Assisi and everything around it. Making it all the way up to Major Rock will be a major accomplishment for a Southern Californian girl who drives more than she walks.

"*Used to* drive more than she walks," I say to myself, proud.

Incredibly, I'm getting stronger by the day. I huff and puff much less on the bike, and when I walk, my leg muscles don't scream obscenities at me as much. I'm still red-faced by the time I reach the piazza, but I'm no longer on the verge of a cardiac event. And, though I've been leisurely exploring Assisi on my way up, I can definitely feel the beginnings of a Franciscan-firm butt. Which is why I stop in at each church—to thank God for the miracle.

Admittedly, I also have my radar out for that boy. The one with the turquoise eyes. Not that his wink meant anything. But you never know. Expanding my Latin education into the Latin *lover* arena would definitely be cool. Or *hot*, if I'm lucky. I have noticed—to my serious joy—that Italian girls have curves. That whole LA Lollipop look never made it across the ocean. Here, having hips isn't considered a mortal sin.

As I pass colorful flower boxes, heavy wood doors, a carved marble fountain with water spitting out from a lion's mouth, I feel *peaceful*. It's freaky. I can't remember the last time I felt so calm in Santa Monica.

Is it the water? The wine? Somehow, it seems as though the very air is different here. Thicker. When you're in it long enough, it's impossible to rush through it. I feel so much more relaxed than I usually do. The black cloud of doom that is normally on my horizon is now the golden glow of beautiful Assisi. Mom would be proud.

"Brava!" I say to myself. Things are looking up.

Twenty-four

"How high today?"

Oops. I've made my first major blunder of the summer. I e-mailed my mother all about my shrinking butt and daily chug-a-lug up the hill. I *didn't* mention the bikini photos of her, or my insights into why she may be overly obsessed with my weight. It felt like an invasion of her privacy to let her know Patrice showed me the photos she banned from our own family albums. Today, though, Mom's free-wheeling romp in the waves feels like a Photoshop trick. Was that really her?

"Does Patrice have a scale?" she IMs me the moment I log on.

"What are you doing up?" I write back.

"Waiting for you, of course," she replies. Then she writes, "If Patrice doesn't have a scale, buy one with the emergency ATM card I gave you."

Only Mom would consider buying a scale an "emergency." My insights fly out the window and bounce through the piazza. Mom and I are back in the same old dance.

"How high did you walk today?" she types. "And are you walking *briskly*?"

"How's Quinn?" I ask, ignoring her question.

"As usual, glued to his Xbox," she replies.

"Dad?"

"Married to his TiVo."

"And you?" I ask.

"Depressed."

My body goes on alert. My mother, Ms. Life Coach, is *never* depressed. *Re*pressed, maybe. But, as she once said, "The only depression you'll see on me is the hollow above my collarbone."

"What's going on, Mom?" I ask, worried.

"Remember my friend Colleen?"

"Yes," I type, afraid to read what happened to Colleen.

"Her daughter got married."

"And?"

"The wedding was a formal sit-down dinner."

"I don't get it, Mom," I write. "What happened to Colleen?"

"Colleen? She's fine. A size *four*! It's *me*. I drank too

132

much wine and fell back into old eating behaviors. I ate prime rib!"

My fingers lie motionless on the keyboard. I'm speechless.

"All my hard work wasted," Mom writes. "The next day, I woke up four pounds heavier."

Thousands of miles away, I can still hear her whimper.

"It's not like you have to go into rehab," I type. "It's only beef."

"Like they say," Mom types, "one bite is too much, a hundred bites are not enough."

I'm tempted to lighten the mood by telling her we're finally having the mother/daughter bonding moment she's always wanted, but my heart isn't in it. Not when my body and I are finally befriending each other. And if I had a talking scale here, it would definitely say, "Looking fine!" in Italian.

Plus, Patrice is right. My perspective is changing. Obsessing over four pounds seems ridiculous when women were once executed on the Hill of Hell just because people thought they were witches.

"Promise me you won't make my mistakes, Hayley."

"Don't worry, Mom. I will *never* make carrot and parsnip curry."

"Ha, ha."

"Gotta go," I write.

"Eat your veggies," she replies.

Quickly, I disconnect.

The moment I'm offline, I feel the rumbling of hunger in my stomach. Suddenly, the thought of a gelato seems like the best idea I've had *ever.*

"Walk it off, Hayley," I say out loud. Two other people in the café stare at me, but I don't care. Some things are too important to keep silent.

Marching out the door, I walk to the far end of the square, past the gelato stand, the town hall, and the fountain. Today, I'm aiming for the church of Saint Rufino. Like I said, there are churches *everywhere.* Supposedly, this one has three awesome rose windows that are a must-see. Taking a deep breath, I lift my head and my right foot and begin my stride up the steep hill.

"This one's for the witches," I say.

Twenty-five

I'm sore this morning, but happy. The sun wakes me up with a warm kiss to the cheek. As I quickly shower and dress, my mind flashes on Drew Wyler. He's so far away, his image is a faded fresco in my mind. Finally, I'm fairly sure I could see him without *feeling* him. My eyes could take him in while my heart kept its distance.

Elated, I practically skip down the spiral staircase to join the De Lucas for breakfast.

"We're out here," Gianna calls from the backyard.

I can tell by her voice that she's excited about something. With Gianna, it could be anything from the formation of a new boy band to capturing a ladybug.

"This is my best friend, Romy," Gianna says, as I join

her in the backyard. "She is from Germany, but she lives in Italy."

"Ah, yes," I say, vaguely remembering Gianna's chatter about her. "Hi there, Romy." I hold out my hand.

Romy seems like the blank canvas to Gianna's full-color portrait. Her hair is white-blond and she wears a beige T-shirt over ivory shorts. Even her skinny legs are pale to the point of looking blue.

Shyly taking my extended hand, Romy limply shakes it, looking at me with a quick sideways glance.

"We have a surprise!" Gianna chirps. Then she's off and running, with Romy scampering behind her.

From the far corner of the De Lucas' enormous backyard, Patrice and Taddeo wave as we all gallop up. They are both standing behind a high fence made of wooden posts and rings of thick wire. Patrice wears a floppy sun hat and gloves. Taddeo is happily covered in dirt. Gino, obviously, is already in Perugia at work.

"Come!" Gianna leads me through a makeshift gate into a lush, colorful garden. Some growth is new, some well-established. Romy gravitates toward the brown-and-yellow sunflowers that loom over her head.

"*Buon giorno*, Hayley," Patrice says, wiping a strand of hair out of her eyes with the back of her glove.

"You are purple!" Taddeo shouts.

Gianna stamps her foot in the soft earth. "I was going to tell her!"

136

"Tell me what?" I ask.

Composing herself, Gianna lifts her head regally and says, "Welcome to the De Luca family garden. *Mamma* is green, Taddeo is yellow, I am red, and now you are purple!"

Grinning, I look around at the tidy garden. Below the sunflowers are clumps of basil, sage, and parsley. Short stalks of fat tomatoes stand next to new stalks of corn. Low to the ground I see fluffy heads of looseleaf lettuce and a sprawling green vine bearing tiny eggplants.

Yellow, green, red, and purple.

"It's a family project," Patrice explains. "Each year we pick a different color to plant and tend. After lunch, before *riposo*, you'll usually find us out here."

"Now with you, too!" Gianna squeals.

"I'm honored," I say. And I am. How cool is this?

Since I live in an apartment back in the States, I've never had a yard. Mom plants flowers in the two window boxes out front, but it's the same red geraniums every year. After a while, I don't even see them. How awful is that? Here, you can't help but notice the life all around you.

Romy gathers a bunch of wildflowers from the edge of the fence while Gianna checks her beets, Taddeo pokes around a row of yellow squash, Patrice clips sprigs of fresh oregano, and I examine several bursting heads of purple lettuce to see what they might need.

Today, I forget about my climb into the Assisi sky and dig my hands into Italian earth.

Twenty-Six

Tonight, it's gin. The card game, not the drink.

"*Grazie,*" Gianna says, scooping up my discard.

"*Prego,*" I reply, looking slyly over my fanned-out cards.

Patrice and Gino are sitting opposite each other in cushioned armchairs behind us. Both read the newspaper. Taddeo is on the floor constructing an elaborate looped track for his Hot Wheels. The scent of roasted garlic still lingers in the air, and on my tongue. I sip decaf espresso, nibble almond biscotti. I reach my hand out to take a new card from the draw pile. Gianna giggles. I can always tell when she's close to declaring gin.

"Not so fast, girly-girl," I say, smiling. I only need one more card to win.

To my utter amazement, I've fallen easily into the De Luca family routine. Their effortlessness with one another has mellowed my soul. No one needs to talk to relate. A blaring television doesn't have to replace conversation. Mostly, in moments of silence, it doesn't feel like there is a flood of words being dammed up. Here, quiet is just that— *quiet*. It's not angry silence or pouting or not listening. This family feels united under one roof, not imprisoned.

Is the difference my family? I wonder. Me? My country? Our lifestyle? Or just the way we choose to live? Seeing my life from a distance of six thousand miles is putting everything in perspective. Here, in the simplicity of Italy, I feel as though I've overcomplicated my life in California. I've lived in my head, not my heart. Even as my heart was being broken, I tried to quickly look past it. Get over it. Suck it up. Did I ever let myself *feel* it? In all the noise of my life, did I even hear my heart cry out?

"I win!" Gianna squeals, slapping down her discard. "We play again?"

I grin. "Okay," I say, surprised at how fun it is to play cards with a ten-year-old. The last game I played with my brother, Quinn, was Monopoly.

"Pay up, sucker!" I said each time he landed on one of my properties.

"You're going to eat it, loser!" he said back to me.

Suddenly, I feel homesick. But it's an odd kind of feeling. My heart aches for a home I've never had.

"I deal," Gianna says.

She beams. It's contagious. My heart twangs again. I feel both sad and happy, longing for the past and excited for the future. My stomach is churning with emotion.

At that moment, in the De Luca living room, while I sort my cards and smile at Gianna, I make a decision. From now on, however I feel, I'm going to feel it. Really *feel* it. Even if it kills me.

Twenty-Seven

It was simple. All I did was say one sentence and *poof!* Last night, while playing gin with Gianna, I mentioned that I'd like to go to Rome. This morning, with the entire De Luca family, here I am. In the car on my way to Roma. It's easy to identify my true feelings today—I'm ecstatic.

"*Vengo ecco!*" I shout. Here I come! At least I *think* that's how you say it. It must be, because everyone in the car bellows it, too.

"*Vengo ecco! Vengo ecco!*"

Gino is driving, since he's taken the day off to join us. I helped Patrice pack a picnic basket earlier, with fresh strawberries from her (our!) garden and prosciutto sandwiches on thinly sliced bread from the *panetteria* up the hill. We're all crammed in the tiny car, but it feels more like an adventure than torture. Gianna, Taddeo, and I are in the backseat; Gino, Patrice, and our lunch feast are in the front.

"Can we climb Mount Vesuvius?" Taddeo asks, clapping his hands.

"It's in Naples, sweetheart," Patrice says, laughing.

"The mountain blowed up," he informs me.

I grin, and flash on my brother. His favorite Xbox game is Crusty Demons. When Dad bought it for his tenth birthday, I was agog.

I read the description out loud. "Spectacular crashes inflict massive injuries and pain to dirt-bike riders. Plus, it's rated 'mature' and we both know Quinn is anything *but*."

Dad shrugged. "Boys will be boys."

In the front seat on the highway to Rome, I see Gino shrug the same way. I guess dads will be dads.

Gino drives as fast as every other Italian. I try not to freak out, or picture spectacular crashes that inflict massive injuries, as he straddles two lanes. Plus, he talks with his hands, so no way am I going to ask him anything until we reach Rome in one piece.

Wide green fields stretch out on either side of the highway. Stone farmhouses pop up here and there, along with small villages and hill towns off in the distance. It's hard to believe we're so close to the cradle of Roman civilization. Whatever that means. I just remember it from European History class. If I'd known I would actually *be* here one day,

I would have paid more attention.

"What is Saint Monica like?" Gianna asks me.

"Who?"

"The city where you live in America," she says.

Oh. *That* saint. I chuckle. It's doubtful anyone who lives in the land of Brazilian butt augmentations even realizes that their city was named after a saint.

"It's next to the Pacific Ocean," I say. "Sunny all the time, full of tan blondes with abs of steel."

"Sounds beautiful." Gianna sighs.

"To me, *that* is beautiful." I point out the window. An elderly woman in a black dress is watering the red poppies that are growing in front of the crumbling stone wall that surrounds her ancient stone house. That's real. It's *life.*

"It's so old!" Gianna moans.

"And everything in Southern California is new. I like old better."

"New is good, too," she says. Gianna quietly curls her fingers around my hand, and again, I get that homesick feeling. When is the last time I reached for Quinn's hand, or he reached for mine?

Rome is about a hundred miles from Assisi, which would take me at least two hours to drive. Barely an hour after we started out, however, Gino announces, *"Roma venti chilometri!"* Rome in twenty kilometers. Which is about twelve miles, I think. I still don't have the conversion right. I screw up euros, too. Is a dollar three-fourths of a euro? Or, is a euro seventy-five cents?

When you look at Rome on a map, it looks like a fried egg. The city is completely encircled by a highway. Vatican City is pretty much the yolk. Gino loops around until he turns left on a street called Via Aurelia.

"All roads lead to Rome," Patrice chirps.

My heart is thrumming. I still can't believe I'm here. In the city where gladiators fought lions, Julius Caesar did *not* invent the Caesar salad, contrary to popular belief, and Renaissance art was born—or *re*born, since the word *renaissance* means *rebirth*. Whoa, I guess I *did* learn something in European History class after all.

Gino drives us down a narrow side street lined with old apartment buildings. In a fast squiggle, he expertly parallel parks.

"Arriviamo!" he declares.

We've arrived. Excited, I climb out of the backseat and stretch, nearly getting creamed by a motorcycle that whizzes past. The driver, a gorgeous Italian guy, shouts something at me. His passenger, an even more gorgeous Italian girl, smiles, shrugs her bare shoulders, and wraps her tan arms tighter around his waist. I don't see any hair on her legs, underarms, *or* upper lip.

As I look around me, I see what the old lady on the plane was talking about. Rome is a bit dirty and smoggy. Traffic is everywhere, and the Romans don't seem to notice it—they drive fast anyway. I can't believe there aren't accidents at every intersection.

Then we turn a corner, and everything changes.

"Saint Peter's square," Gino says, opening his arms like a proud papa. The center of the Catholic church.

Wow. The square surrounding the yolk. Which isn't a *square* at all. With my mouth hanging open, I walk through the wide opening and step back in time. The huge round piazza has large stone pillars all around it, four deep. People are everywhere. Some praying, some taking photographs. It's easy to spot the first-timers—their jaws are gaping open too.

On top of the columns, standing like gray cypress trees, are statues of all the saints. Of course, I'm dying to find my fave—Saint Francis of Assisi. Taddeo takes my hand and drags me to the right side.

"*Qui,*" he says.

Francis is so high in the air, I can barely see him. Yet I can still make out the image of a man I've seen depicted all over Assisi—pious, kind, saintly. With my hand still in his, Taddeo pulls me past the obelisk in the center of the "square," the Pope's apartment, and the building with the famous balcony where the Pope is always sitting and waving.

"This is Vatican City," Patrice says. "Its own little country smack in the middle of Rome."

"Is that the Pope's private church?" I ask, pointing to the huge domed building at the opposite end of the circle.

Patrice laughs. "I guess so. Though he lets lots of us in.

Saint Peter's Basilica is one of the largest churches in the world. Sixty *thousand* people can attend mass there."

We walk inside the gargantuan church. Sunlight glows softly through the windows of the impossibly high dome. Curved ceilings all around are gold and shimmering. The altar is framed by a giant bronze structure that looks like a pagoda. I wonder if Dante once stood where I'm standing now. Did he look up at the heavenly ceiling and imagine what it was like in hell?

Instead of sitting on one of the pews in the center of the church, we stroll along the edge. The first sight is the most heartbreaking sculpture I've ever seen.

"Michelangelo's *Pietà*," Patrice says quietly. "He carved this when he was just twenty-four years old."

The shiny gray sculpture—the body of Jesus draped over his devastated mother's lap—sits behind glass.

"A crazy guy with a sledgehammer came in here in the seventies and hacked off Mary's arm and part of her nose," Patrice says.

I gasp. "Who could do such a thing?"

"Who could deliberately fly a plane into a building?" Patrice replies. "The world is full of insanity."

Quietly, we exit out the side and circle around to the most famous building in Vatican City: the Sistine Chapel. There's a line to get in, but I don't mind waiting. It's a warm, sunny day and Gianna entertains me with a spot-on imitation of Madonna singing "Like a Virgin."

Gino, of course, is mortified. *"Silenzio,"* he commands. *"Rispetto."* Gianna instantly shuts her mouth.

The Sistine Chapel is definitely worth the wait. I can't believe human beings could create such beauty. The room is a rectangle, with a long arched ceiling. All the best painters were hired to create it—Botticelli, Rosselli, Perugino, and, of course, Buonarroti, who's better known by his first name: Michelangelo. Like Cher.

"Four years on his back in the air," Gino says, as we all gape at the vibrant colors of so many famous images. Especially the most famous: God and man touching fingers.

Did Michelangelo know he was creating art that would inspire millions of people for centuries? He *had* to know. How could you not?

Once again, I'm struck by the difference between museums at home and here. When the Getty Center opened in Los Angeles, my parents took us there on the freeway.

"Five dollars to park!" Dad had groaned.

"Let's see the famous paintings first," Mom had said, "so we can make it home for lunch."

There, the museum was a destination, a trip, a building so high on a hill you had to take a tram to reach it. Here, you turn a corner and art washes over you. With each step, you go back hundreds of years. In some parts of Rome, *thousands* of years.

"I hungry," Taddeo says. I laugh. Yeah, boys everywhere will be boys.

Though it's close to lunchtime, we have one more stop before we eat. Flagging a taxi outside Vatican City, Gino tells the driver where to go in Italian. Off we go, snaking through traffic at heart-stopping speed. My knuckles are white on the armrest. Patrice, next to me, pats my knee.

"Close your eyes," she suggests. But I don't. Even though Rome is flying past, I don't want to miss a single sight.

We drive over the Tiber River, careen down one wide street and several narrow ones, until the car lurches to a halt.

"Il Pantheon!" the driver announces proudly, as if he built it himself.

Thrilled I made it alive, I'm even more psyched to see another building I'd learned about in my European History class. The Pantheon. One of the *ancient* structures in Rome. Built by the Roman Empire, it's been standing for centuries.

Inside, I look up to see the biggest brick dome in the history of architecture. Patterned like a waffle, I'm dwarfed beneath it. But the coolest thing of all is the open circle at the very top. The whole dome is a *sundial*, with the sunlight coming through marking time at the base of the dome as the day passes. The most amazing thing is it still tells perfect time.

"Lunchtime!" Gino announces, looking up at the massive sundial.

We laugh and follow him outside. In the warm Roman air, I stop to take my emotional temperature. I smile and sigh. I feel utterly, completely, totally *content.*

A short walk later, the De Lucas and I are in the Piazza Navona, Rome's beautiful main square. Which, of course, isn't square, either—it's a huge oval, with three fountains and hundreds of people eating lunch. We find a spot in the shade of the most stunning sculpture: the Fountain of the Four Rivers, which has men who seem to climb out of the rock itself.

What must it be like to live with such beauty? I wonder. Do the Romans appreciate it? Or is it like the Southern Californian coastline at sunset? Beautiful, yes. But ho-hum when you see it every day.

"Mangia!"

I help Patrice pass out the sandwiches we made that morning, while Gino opens the bottle of wine. The kids drink sparkling water. With the first bite, my tastebuds rejoice. Prosciutto that's dry and salty and incredibly delicious. I chew slowly, let the flavors invade my whole mouth. Between bites, I nibble on home-grown strawberries that taste so sweet and tart I feel as though I've never eaten a real strawberry before. I sip the earthy red wine. I feel like a Roman goddess.

Me. Hayley. The chubby girl with the pretty face. Today, I feel beautiful.

The rest of the afternoon and early evening is a walk through history. It's almost too much to absorb in one day. I'm on sensory overload. First, the ancient Colosseum, where gladiators fought and crowds cried for blood. It's strange to see such a familiar ruin so close to modern apartment buildings and hotels. Beyond the Colosseum are the remains of the Forum. Though a lot of it has crumbled, you can almost see the Romans meeting there in their togas to shop, go to the bank, listen to public speakers.

"Like Times Square in New York," Gianna says.

By the time the sun begins to fade, we've all faded, too. Taddeo is asleep in his mother's arms. We decide to have an early supper in a nearby trattoria, then head home. Sounds good to me. I'm wiped out. I also can't wait to get up tomorrow morning and hike up to the Internet café to tell Jackie all about my amazing day.

"What you want to eat?" Gino asks me.

My answer is one word: "Pancetta!"

When in Rome . . .

Twenty-Eight

The spirit of Italy has taken over my soul. I'm relaxed, happy, warm. It's as if I'm part of the earth, not just standing on it. Today, the sun is a soft blanket around my body. It feels good. I'm up early, so Jackie won't have to stay up so late. My legs are pedaling joyfully to the bottom of Assisi's big hill. My shorts are loose, my thighs feel tight. It's been two days since I connected with Jackie. Once, that would have made me crazy, but now I'm on Italian time. Nothing is rushed; everything happens when it's supposed to.

A horse, grazing in the green field to my right, flips his mane at me. I flip my mane right back. Cycling past an old woman in her garden, I shout, *"Buon giorno!"* She waves and returns the greeting.

With my bike locked in the parking lot at the bottom of the hill, I begin my now-familiar ascent to the Internet café. Shop owners know me by now. The florist plucks one of his yellow daisies and gives it to me as a gift.

"Grazie," I say, tucking the stem behind my ear.

Something is happening to me. I'm accepting myself more. Maybe it's seeing the ruins of Rome and realizing how briefly we're on this planet. Or maybe it's just Italy itself. From here, Southern California seems like a mirage. Why have I spent so many years obsessing over fitting into a mirage?

Mario, the guy behind the counter at the Internet café, brings me an espresso without having to be asked. He says, "Computer number three is free."

I sit in front of the screen, stir a packet of sugar into my espresso, take a sip, then log in to see if Jackie is online.

"Helloooooooo," I type. "U up?"

After a few moments and another sip of the hot, strong espresso, an IM pops up on the screen.

"Hi," it says simply.

Thrilled to "talk" to my best friend, my fingers fly across the keyboard. I describe Rome, pancetta, the horse that morning, and my new sense of inner peace. If anyone can understand my transformation, it's Jackie.

"Wuz up w/u?" I ask finally.

The screen is blank. I wait. I see that she's still online. Did she leave to get a coffee? Go to the bathroom?

"Jackie???"

My heart stops when the next three words appear on my screen.

"Drew is here."

Both hands fly up to my mouth. I can't believe my eyes. Then, of course, I can. Has he been there all along? Is this the first time she's had the guts to tell me?

Bliss drains from my body like *sangue* from a punctured heart.

Trying to be cool, I type, "Yo, D. Wuz up?"

My chest feels like a cannonball just hit it. I try to take a deep breath, but it hurts.

"I'm good." Drew gets on Jackie's computer and IMs me. "Howz IT?"

"Hot," I write. "And cool. Howz ur sumr?"

"Same ole shit."

I'm dying to ask, "What are you doing there? It's late. Did you and Jackie just have sex? Do you ever think of me at all?"

Instead, I write, "Hanging at the beach?"

He replies, "We're going tomorrow."

The cannonball hits again. Lower. This time, a shot to the gut. *We.* Jackie and Drew are already a "we"?

My Italian ease dissolves into American heartache. Just when I thought I was fine.

"Time's up," I type quickly. "Say bye 4 me."

I disconnect before Jackie has the chance to get back on.

"Another espresso?" Mario asks.

"No, *grazie*," I say, paying fast and nearly running out the door.

For the first time since I've arrived in Italy, I find a phone booth at the corner of the square and call Patrice.

"I won't be home for lunch," I say, tossing the stupid daisy behind my ear to the ground.

"You okay?" she asks.

"Yeah," I lie. "I feel like staying in town today."

"Be sure to eat something, Hayley."

"Don't worry. I will."

On autopilot, I hang up the phone and walk halfway down the hill to the pastry shop I've passed every day. Thank God it's still open. The glass shelves in the window are piled high with biscotti, meringues, chocolate squares, and pistachio cookies.

Inside, the smell of baking dough and melted butter fills my head as I inhale hard. I say, *"Parla inglese?"*

"A little," the woman behind the counter replies.

"I need a bag full of different pastries for a party tonight," I say.

She looks confused. *"Desidera . . . ,"* she says, pointing to different plates in the glass display case, *"questo?"*

"Sì," I say. Then I point to others. *"E questo, e questo, e questo."* Even though she doesn't understand me, I feel compelled to add, "There will be lots of people there. I need enough for everyone."

The total is a whopping twenty-two euros. The bulging bag weighs a ton. My heart weighs even more. I thank the woman, leave the store, and climb back up the hill. I'm not sure where I'm going, but I'll know it when I get there. A place to hide.

Down a tiny, shaded side street, I find the perfect spot. An old stone building is being renovated. Was it damaged in the earthquake, I wonder? No one is working there today, though it's covered in scaffolding. A low scaffold, around the side of the building, makes a perfect bench. No one will see me here.

I sit, open the pastry bag, and devour several marzipan cookies before I even realize what I'm doing. I barely taste them. But soon, I *feel* them.

"Good," I say out loud.

My emotions can take a hike. Right now, I need to feel full.

Twenty-Nine

"Is something wrong, honey?" Patrice asks me.

We're working in the garden, but my heart isn't in it. The purple section is all droopy. Like me.

"I'm fine," I say, my sharp tone letting her know not to ask me again. In yet another way she's nothing like my mom, Patrice leaves it alone.

For the next several days, I don't go anywhere. I sleep a lot, eat too much. After lunch, I do the dishes. Before dinner, I poke around the garden. As soon as I can, I go straight to the top of my tower. Even Gianna seems afraid to bother me. After supper one evening, she slips a note under my closed bedroom door.

"We play gin tonight?"

"No, *grazie*," I write, slipping the note back under.

I want to be left alone. The De Lucas don't push me. In fact, through my open window one evening, I hear Gino say, "She know we here, if she need us. Let her live her own life."

Since he said it in English, I know he wanted me to hear. I was going to shout "Thank you," from my window, but when I examined my true feelings, I didn't feel like getting up from my bed.

Every night, just outside my window, that damn hawk cries. Tonight, it's dark, late. I lay flat on my pillow, tears rolling into my hair. I know I'm being stupid. I gave Jackie the green light! Why, then, was it such a blow to hear that she went forward? Why does my heart feel so flattened?

All night, I wallow in my misery. I don't suck it up; I let it out. I *feel* it. Like a shroud, I drape my pain over my entire body. By the time the sun rises, my red eyes are puffy and I barely have the energy to climb down the spiral staircase to breakfast.

I feel like a Roman ruin.

I'm crumbled—the Forum, not the Pantheon. I'm only half here.

Suddenly, I flash on the beautiful, sunny day I spent in Rome. Midway down the staircase, I stop. My head fills with images. The original Saint Peter's Church was destroyed and was rebuilt, the Colosseum was damaged by earthquakes, yet it still stands strong. Even in Assisi, they've picked up the pieces of fallen frescoes and restored their beauty. Why am I so fragile that I fall to pieces over one Instant Message?

"Why, Hayley?" I ask out loud, standing outside on my stairs.

I hear Ms. Antonucci's voice in my head. *Memorize every moment.*

Then I hear Gino. *Live your own life.*

I don't need to hear any more.

"Basta," I say. "Enough."

Experiencing my emotions is one thing. Feeling sorry for myself the rest of the summer, and eating my way into a Colosseum-sized ass, is quite another. It's time to get *off* my ass and experience life.

"No more pouting!" I say, raising my chin. "Lift yourself up!"

Instantly, my destiny unfolds before me. I know just what I'm going to do.

"Hayley," I say out loud. "Today you go straight to the top."

Thirty

Nothing's going to stop me. My sunscreen is on, my water bottle is full. I'm wearing two peds on each foot for extra cushioning, and my hair is braided and twirled in a tight knot on top of my head. I ate a good breakfast, rode the bike leisurely to what I now call "base camp" at the bottom of Assisi's huge hill. I've already told Patrice not to expect me for lunch. I have no idea how long it will take. But I don't care. No matter what, I'm going to reach Major Rock today. The Fortress. The top.

"Adrian!" I screech in a lame imitation of Rocky Balboa. Tourists, as well as locals, stare. But it's okay. Today, I'm on my way to living my *own* life.

The flower shop is open, as are the souvenir, soap, and

pastry shops. Briskly, I walk straight past, waving as I go. Pumping my arms, I maintain a good pace. The piazza is bustling, but I don't stop there, either. I pass the Temple of Minerva and the clock tower. Wiping my damp forehead on my sleeve, I keep walking.

There isn't a cloud in the sky. The stone buildings are almost white in the Umbrian sun. It's impossibly beautiful. My heart still aches, but at the same time, it soars.

I have no idea exactly where I'm going . . . other than up. I'm hoping there will be signs to point the way. The higher I ascend the stone sidewalk, the fewer people are with me. As I pass the churches I've already visited, I feel my blood pumping furiously. Still, I don't slow down. I can't. Even if it kills me.

"Fa molto caldo," a woman says to me as she stands outside her home on the hill, watering her flowers.

Not understanding her, I smile and shrug. She points to the hot sun.

"Ah, *sì, sì,*" I say. It must be universal. Even in Italy, strangers talk to one another about the weather.

Finally, just before the Church of Saint Rufino, I see a sign and a drawing pointing to Rocca Maggiore. The road to Major Rock is a sharp U-turn up an even steeper hill. Stopping for a moment to catch my breath, I look down at the beautiful Umbrian valley. My mind flashes on Jackie and Drew, but I shut my eyes and block them out. Today, on the road to the top, I refuse to let anything bring me down.

Since it's getting close to lunchtime, my stomach rumbles. I doubt there's a trattoria up at the old fortress, but I'm hoping for a food cart, panini stand—*something*. Admittedly, I didn't plan this very well. I should have brought lunch with me.

"Oh well, Hayley," I say, smiling. "Your body will just have to burn the fuel you store in your thighs."

Up ahead, there is a long, multitiered staircase. Made of gray brick, with a skinny black wrought-iron handrail, it extends so far I can't see the top. Major Rock, here I come.

Inhaling, and tucking strands of hair behind my ears, I start up. I stop once for water, once more to breathe. Halfway up, my calves ache, my chest heaves, and my sunscreen has completely slithered off my face. I look like a marathon runner who's determined to cross the finish line no matter how late it is. Which, I sort of am. At least the determination part.

At last, like a mirage in the desert, I see a gate, an arch, and—thank God!—a café. Still not at Major Rock, at least I can stop and eat and get some feeling back in my legs.

"Buon giorno," a short, stout woman behind the counter greets me. Her café is a tiny brown snack shack tucked into the trees. Empty plastic tables and chairs circle the small brick square outside. If not for the flowers planted along the edges, the scene would totally creep me out. It's isolated and deserted. Major horror flick potential. *Murder of the Hungry*

Tourist. The one with the pretty face.

"Parla inglese?" I ask the woman, though I know what her answer will be. This high feels like I'm in another country.

She holds her index finger up as if to say, "Just a sec," and calls to the back room. "Lorenzo!"

A swinging door pushes open and my heart leaps onto the brick floor. It's *him*. The boy with the turquoise eyes.

"Americana!" he says.

Though I didn't think it possible, my red cheeks get redder. My hair is plastered to my head, my bare face is freckled by the sun. I don't even have lip gloss on! I've never looked worse. Yet, here he is, standing in front of me, grinning. The gap between his two front teeth makes my knees wobble.

"Sit anywhere you like," he says. "I save all the tables for you."

I laugh and grab the nearest seat outside. Between the uphill climb and his wine-colored lips, I can't trust my legs to hold me up much longer.

"What you like?" he asks.

All I can think of are three words: You, you, you.

Thirty-One

"Call me Enzo," he says, pronouncing his name as if there's a "t" in it: *Ent-zo.*

"Call me Hayley," I reply, knowing his pronunciation will drop the "h."

Ayley and Entzo. I like the sound of that.

It's cool in the shade at the outdoor table. A breeze caresses my face. I'm still damp all over, but now it's more nerves than exertion.

"I'll have, um, a salad," I order. "Small."

Enzo laughs. "No salad. Espresso?"

"No espresso. Panini?" I ask.

"No panini. *Momento.*"

Enzo disappears into the food shack, then reappears

with two ice-cream cones.

"Gelato!" he says with such joy I don't have the heart to refuse.

Chill out, Hayley, I say to myself. You can handle one ice-cream cone without going berserk.

"*Grazie,*" I say. The ice cream is already beginning to melt.

It's raspberry. As I lick the drip that's rolling down the cone, and take a mouthful of gelato, my whole body melts. It's as if I've never tasted ice cream before, or raspberries. Real fresh raspberries are crushed into the thick, creamy, vanilla ice cream. The rich, soft texture is like eating cold silk.

"You like?" Enzo asks.

"I love," I say.

Suddenly remembering my manners, I ask, "Would you like to sit down?"

Enzo sits. Completely relaxed, he leans back in the plastic chair and enjoys his gelato. I can't take my eyes off him. I try, but they keep shifting back. He twirls the cone in a circle as he licks it. A small drip lands on his chin. His tongue, like a gecko's, shoots out and scoops it up. His smooth brown neck undulates with each swallow.

"My first gelato," I say, unable to think of anything more intelligent.

"My first *Americana*," he replies.

I blush. What does he mean by *that*? Enzo smiles, and I

smile back, my pulse throbbing. I force myself not to devour the ice cream. No way am I going to polish off my cone first. Enzo's thick black hair dances all over his head. He's wearing a striped polo shirt, open at the collar. His cut-off shorts reveal hairy legs, but the soft curls look so fluffy I long to run my hand down his calf. And that gap in his teeth is almost unbearable. I wonder if you can feel it when you kiss him.

"You go to Rocca Maggiore?" he asks finally.

"Sì," I say.

"It close by the time you get there."

"Oh," I say, startled once again by this country's odd hours.

"Come early tomorrow. We go together, no?"

Climb Mount Everest again? Get up early, double my peds, sweat my way to the top?

"I'd love to," I say.

Enzo grins and I fall hopelessly into that glorious gap.

I meant to e-mail Jackie. Really, I did. It's just that I floated down the hill in a daze. Straight past the piazza and the Internet café. I don't even remember pedaling my bike from base camp back to my tower. Somehow, I just arrived home. In time for lunch, of course.

"I had my first gelato," I announced dreamily.

Gianna asked, "Can I braid your hair?"

Thirty-Two

I'm awake the moment the sun illuminates Assisi. I jump out of bed, cross the stone floor, and gaze out the window. It's the most striking sight I've ever seen. Except for Enzo's neck. The whole city is pink. I look up at Major Rock, and imagine Enzo waking up. Does he live in the back of that shack? Is his home that high on the hill?

Showering and dressing quickly, I eat breakfast with the De Lucas and tell Patrice I won't be home for lunch.

"Something I should know?" she asks, raising both eyebrows.

"Not yet," I answer, skipping out the door.

Today, I'm wearing beige capri pants, a white T-shirt, and sneakers. My clothes are tighter than they were a week ago, but I haven't done too much damage. It's not too late to turn things around. My hair is pulled back with a claw clip, but I've let a few tendrils fall to soften the look. They'll probably be strings of wet hair by the time I reach the top of the brick staircase, but my last look in the mirror doesn't make me gag. In fact, I actually look pretty good. Instead of plain sunscreen, I've applied tinted moisturizer with SPF 15. My lashes are swiped with waterproof mascara, and my lips are kissably plump with a frosty cherry gloss I bought in Santa Monica before I left.

"No jokes," I instruct myself aloud as I cycle toward Assisi. No way am I going to repeat the mistake I made with Drew. I don't need another *friend*. It's time to stop being the funny girl with the pretty face. I'm going to reinvent myself. From now on, I'm the seductress with the hourglass bod.

The sun makes me chuckle as I lock my bike and head up the hill. Perfect days like this in Santa Monica drove me nuts. Why couldn't it ever rain? Why was everyone always wearing sleeveless camis? Here, in beautiful Assisi, the sun is a loving embrace. Here, the sunlight is used to grow flowers, grapes, olives—not just to show off trainer-made biceps and spray-on tans.

Now that the path is familiar, it doesn't take long to make my way to the staircase. Still, I'm panting when I get there. At the bottom, I stop to catch my breath and reapply gloss. Then, I take my first step into destiny. From the first moment I gazed into Enzo's eyes, I was moving toward this moment. I didn't know it, but I was.

"Ayley!"

"Entzo!"

He kisses both my cheeks and I inhale his musky scent. It's like a walk in the forest.

"Come va?" I ask, in my most seductive voice—as alluring as "How are you?" can get.

"Meet my *mamma*," he replies.

His mother? We haven't even had a first date and already I'm meeting the parents? My heart instantly thumps.

Enzo's mother is the woman I saw yesterday behind the counter. She looks older than my mom, but maybe it's the belted dress and pantyhose. Or the graying hair and flat black shoes. Enzo speaks to her in Italian, and she embraces me and erupts in a flood of words I don't understand. Then, she reaches behind the counter and pulls out a picnic basket.

"Il pranzo," she says. A phrase I've come to know well. Lunch!

Enzo takes the basket in one hand, and my arm in the other. His touch sends sparks through my body.

"Ciao, Mamma," Enzo says.

"Ciao," I say, too.

Then, we're out the door and on our way up.

"I was afraid you no come," Enzo says shyly.

"I was in the neighborhood," I quip.

Enzo laughs, and I wince. *No jokes!*

"I'm glad to be here," I say, amending my comment. Lowering my voice an octave, I add, "with you."

"I happy to be with you, too," he replies, and my knees turn to gelato.

Rocca Maggiore is an ancient sand-colored castle rising into the cobalt blue sky above Assisi. Like the other medieval buildings I've seen, it seems to grow out of the earth itself. Few tourists are all the way up here. Most stop at Saint Francis's church or the piazza. I'm so glad I finally made it. The view is spectacular. Stretching out far below—like a soft green quilt—is the entire Tiber Valley.

"My country," Enzo says proudly.

Despite my protest, Enzo pays for our admission, and we enter the dark, cool fortress. As if I haven't climbed high enough already, there are two soaring towers to ascend. The tallest is reached only by a creepy passageway and narrow, murky staircase.

"We go up," Enzo says, gripping our lunch basket in one hand, the railing in the other.

They give us flashlights, which I hold and point, but it makes the climb even more spooky as our shadows dance along the stone walls. It smells like mud. Plus, it's impossible not to feel totally claustrophobic. But no way am I going to wimp out. Not when I've come this far.

Once I reach the top, and we're out in the air again, it's clear to see it was all worth it. The sun is bright, but the air is cool. We're alone on the top of the world. Amazingly, I feel calm. My mother would go werewolf on me if she knew I was alone with a boy I didn't know. Especially this high in the air. I doubt I'd do it in Los Angeles. I've seen *Forensic Files*. I know the crazed things people can do to one another. But with Enzo, I don't get a danger vibe at all. It must be Italy. Or maybe it's the fact that I *haven't* been watching *Forensic Files* lately. The notion that everyone is a potential serial killer has faded in the Italian sun.

"Where did you learn English?" I ask him.

"School. Tourists. American movies. I want to speak better."

For the gazillionth time since I landed in Italy, I'm struck by another difference between our countries. If someone walked up to me on the Santa Monica Promenade and asked, "Do you speak Italian?" I'd laugh. Maybe that's why the world hates us. We think we're all *that*. Like the whole world *ought* to speak our language even though we don't speak theirs.

"I'm sorry I don't know Italian," I say. "I wish I did."

"It's cool," he says, grinning. "I'm down with that."

I laugh. "Your American movies are hip-hop?"

He sings, "It's hard out there for a pimp," from the movie *Hustle and Flow*. I laugh again. Statue of Liberty, Monica Lewinsky, Big Macs, and pimps. We definitely need better PR.

Enzo's turquoise eyes twinkle. His black lashes nearly

curl onto themselves. I swallow hard.

"Your parents own the café?" I ask, careful not to call his family business a "shack."

"Only my mother. My father is died."

"I'm sorry."

"He was sick for long time," Enzo says. "He die years ago. I was sad for so long. Now, it is my normal."

"It's just you and your mom?"

"My older brother at university in Perugia. My mother and I run café."

"Is she okay alone today?" I ask.

Enzo nods. "When I'm gone, our neighbors help if many people come."

Another difference between our two countries. Or maybe it's just my family and Southern California. The only time I see my neighbors is at the mailbox, and they usually greet me suspiciously, like maybe I'm spying on them to ruin their sweet rent-control deal. Or maybe, I think suddenly, it's *me*. Have I been so closed off, my neighbors don't want to say hi?

"What is your normal?" Enzo asks, bringing me back to the present.

Laughing, I say, "I don't have a normal. I have two crazy parents and a weird little brother." Then I stop, berating myself for slamming my parents when Enzo doesn't even have a dad. He saves me by saying, "My brother is also crazy and my mother is sometimes weird."

We laugh together. Enzo is easy to talk to, even though his English is spotty and my Italian is nonexistent. Italian time ticks differently than American time. It's slower, yet hours seem to pass quickly. Enzo and I sit on top of the tower together—not saying much, but feeling everything—until they kick us out of the tower for the lunchtime closing.

"We have lunch on the mountain," he suggests.

Outside the castle, there's a stone bench overlooking the valley. Together, we sit, open the picnic basket, and pull out the Umbrian feast his mom made. Artichokes in olive oil, prosciutto, peaches, tangy Parmesan cheese, and Cokes. I'm glad there's no wine. Even though I drink a little with the De Lucas, I'm not ready to go it alone. Especially when "alone" means Enzo's lips are only two feet away. I don't want to do something stupid, like fling myself at him too soon. I'd much rather catch him gracefully when he flings himself at me.

Taking small bites, I eat daintily. I practice channeling the Olsen twins. I taste every delicious flavor.

"Is your family rich Americans?" Enzo asks.

"No."

"My family is poor in euro, but rich in love."

"Mine is poor in dollars, but rich in Happy Meal coupons. At least we were before my mother found tofu."

"Tofu?"

"Don't ask."

He says, "Americans say they are poor when they have

everything. Italians are poor only when they have nothing."

Enzo's words make me stop and think. My family has three cars, Quinn has the latest Xbox, I have a new iPod, we live close to the beach, my brother and I have our own rooms, my parents paid for me to fly to Italy. Enzo tells me he lives with his mother in the back of the tiny café. They don't own a car or a computer. They've never left Italy.

"I guess I am a rich American," I say.

Biting into the sweet, juicy peach his mother packed, Enzo says, "I am rich Italian, too."

I have no idea what time it is. We eat and we talk for hours. The sun is fading. *Riposo* must be over soon. I don't want this day—or this date—to end.

"I take you for ride someday on Vespa?" Enzo says.

"Vespa?" I ask.

"Little motorcycle."

"How little?" I ask. "I have a Harley-sized butt."

You idiot! I scream in my head. *No jokes!*

Laughing, Enzo says, "You're funny," and my heart sinks. Here we go again. How could I have slipped back into being my old self?!

Reaching up to run one finger along my warm cheek, Enzo quietly says, "You have beautiful body of woman."

My eyes instantly flood with tears.

"I sorry," he says. "I say wrong thing?"

I shake my head no. For the first time, a boy's words are exactly right.

Thirty-Three

Enzo doesn't have a computer; I don't have a phone.

"Don't worry," he said as he kissed both of my cheeks, "I find you."

They are the most romantic three words I've ever heard.

The morning after our lunch at Major Rock, I couldn't stop smiling. I invited Gianna into my room and listened to her chatter for hours. On the second and third day, I strolled the streets of Assisi hoping to bump into him. After lunch with the De Lucas, I daydreamed about him as I watered the eggplant growing in the garden. By the fourth day, I was considering a hike back up the staircase to the café. But I decided to wait one day more. Then another. Then two. No need to act too slutty. Not yet. After a week had passed, all I could think about was salami, and how good it would taste piled extra high on flatbread with cheese.

What's wrong with me? Why doesn't anyone want me?

"Come to Bastia Umbra with the kids and me," Patrice says this morning. I'm sitting in the kitchen, twirling a tiny spoon around and around in my espresso. "It's just a regular town," she says, "but I need to do some shopping."

"Okay," I say. Why not? What else have I got to do? Enzo has forgotten me. Jackie's probably at the beach with Drew. The whole world is paired off, but me. A giant Noah's ark, with one girl—the girl with the pretty face—flailing in the water alone.

"Can I buy platform sandals, Mamma?" Gianna asks, next to me in the backseat.

"No," Patrice says, as we drive down the long, gravel path to the gate.

The gate slowly opens, and Patrice drives through.

"Who that?" Taddeo asks.

I look up. There, in a big round helmet, on a small red Vespa, is Enzo. He waves and says, "My friend, Stefano, tell me American girl stay here. I hope it is you."

"It is!" Gianna chirps.

"We go for ride?" he asks me.

I catch Patrice's narrowed eyes in the rearview mirror.

"This is my friend, Enzo," I say to Patrice. "Enzo, this is the family I live with for the summer. Patrice, Gianna, and Taddeo."

Gianna giggles, Taddeo says something in Italian, and Patrice stuns me by asking Enzo, "You're Carmina's son, no?"

"You know my *mamma*?"

"We met last year at the feast of Saint Clare. You were there, too."

"Ah, *sì*. Signora De Luca!"

"*Sì.*"

My jaw hanging, I watch Patrice and Enzo get reacquainted. Gianna whispers, *"Che bello!"* in my ear, which I'm pretty sure means, "What a hottie!" Even with a helmet on, it's easy to see that Enzo is gorgeous. Unfortunately, nothing even close to that describes me today. My hair is stringy, my sunscreen is greasy, and my cherry gloss is up the spiral staircase in my bathroom. Why, of all days, today?

Finally, Patrice says, "Give my best to your *mamma*, Enzo. And take care of our girl."

It takes me a moment to realize she's talking about me. Finally, Patrice turns her head and asks, "You going to just sit there, Hayley?"

"Oh!"

With the grace of a rhino extracting itself from a mud hole, I rise out of the backseat. I casually smooth my hair, but it's a lost cause. Thankfully, Enzo hands me a helmet.

"Have fun," Patrice shouts as she drives off.

Standing there with Enzo, looking like a lightbulb in the white helmet, I attempt a casual slouch.

"Nice to see you," I say. Even I can hear the hurt in my voice.

Enzo doesn't offer any explanation. Not that he should. He said we'd go for a ride "someday." How could he possibly know that my translation was "tomorrow" while his was "in a week"? Even in Italy, boy time and girl time are different!

"My Harley," Enzo says, grinning, patting the microscopic patch of seat on the back of his Vespa. An image of myself slipping off at the first bump flashes through my brain. Will he notice I'm gone? Will I end up as roadkill?

"Great!" I say, too loud.

"I go slow," Enzo says. With that, I climb on, *hold* on, and we're off.

Umbria is at its most beautiful, I discover, when the warm wind is stroking your face. Enzo quickly leaves the main road and we ride down narrow lanes, past barking dogs and flower-dotted fields. The air smells of wild onions. My arms are wrapped tightly around Enzo's narrow waist; my thighs press in on his. Shutting my eyes, I rest my cheek on his back and inhale his amazing scent.

We ride forever, it seems. Up into the foothills, down past local vineyards. But I'm on Italian time. I have no idea if hours have passed or minutes. I just know I don't want to stop.

After passing through several small villages and below

old towns tucked into mountains, Enzo slows down and pulls over at the bottom of a wide, gently sloping hill of grass. Beyond it, in the distance, is an old, arched bridge.

"Ponte delle Torri," he says. "Bridge of the Towers. We walk across. Very beautiful."

"Walk across?" I ask, swallowing. The skinny bridge looks like it's at least two hundred feet in the air and three times as long. It spans a deep gorge between two old towns.

"You like."

"You promise?"

Revving up the Vespa, Enzo takes off for the hill town ahead, while I hold on—*hang* on for dear life—as the incline gets steep.

We're in Spoleto, he soon tells me, which reminds me a lot of Assisi. Not as beautiful, but it's still a stunning medieval grouping of stone buildings tucked into a hill. There's a main church (of course) and a town square (of course). As we slowly ride the Vespa up, I miss the sight of Franciscan monks wandering through the piazza. Spoleto's population seems younger, hipper. Even the tourists wear high-heeled sandals.

When we finally get to the top of the town, Enzo parks the Vespa behind a gargantuan gray fortress.

"Italian Alcatraz," he says.

"It's a prison?" I ask.

"Once. Now no more. Like Alcatraz."

The walled fort is flanked by two high towers. Which is

how the bridge, directly behind it, got its name.

Before I remove my helmet, I silently pray to Saint Francis: "If you can do anything about helmet hair, I'd really appreciate it." But I doubt it will work. For starters, he's hardly the Patron Saint of Good Hair Days with that shiny cue ball on top of his head. And, from what I can make out, he was known for being completely *un*vain. He would never get hair plugs or that black hair spray I've seen on late-night TV that "paints" your bald spot away.

"Come, Ayley." Enzo is already walking toward the bridge. His hair—along with everything else about him—looks great. Mine is a flattened mass of dead skin cells. Sucking it up, and sucking everything moveable on my body *in*, I join my beautiful tour guide at one end of the most gorgeous bridge I've ever seen. Golden brown, with high arches beneath the ancient walkway that make it look delicate. But, as Enzo explains, it's been standing since the Bronze Age.

Together, we walk across. High above the forest below.

"What's it like living in a country so full of history?" I ask.

"Sad," he answers. "The world comes to visit, but no one stays."

Thirty-Four

I'm totally lost. I don't have a clue. Each time I see Enzo, my insides sizzle like sunlight dancing on the ocean. I obsess over him when I'm not with him, can't take my eyes off him when I am. Is this love? Lust? Some trick Italian oxygen is playing on my body?

There's one person who can advise me. The moment I log on, she's there.

"WHERE HV U BEEN????"

I sigh. My fingers rest on the keyboard. What can I say? The truth? Drew's use of the word "we" sent me into a tail-spin? I crashed and burned until Enzo put out that fire and lit another?

"Family trip," I lie. "No DSL."

"Swear?" Jackie isn't so easily convinced.

"*Sì.*"

I'm not positive, but I don't think it's a *true* lie if it's in a foreign language.

Jackie buys it. "TNK GD!" she types. "Thought u were mad at me."

"Mad? Y?"

"Drew."

Sadly, I don't know enough Italian to lie my way further. Might as well try the truth.

"I wz jealous. OK now."

"Swear?"

"Yes."

"It's not serious," Jackie writes. "We're just hanging out."

"Does D know that?"

"*Sì.*"

Is Jackie familiar with the foreign language clause in our honesty policy? I let it go. I have other pressing matters at hand.

"I'm in luv," I type. "I think."

"AAAAAHHHHHHH!!!"

My fingers fly as I tell her about Enzo. The shack. His eyes. His *mamma*, his scent, his accent. Finally, I end with our walk across the Bridge of the Towers, and back again. We held hands and said nothing and let the beauty around us fill our hearts.

"That's luv, right?" I ask.

"Or a sappy chick flick," she replies.

Chuckling, I type, "What the flick do I do now?????"

Jackie types five words, all in caps.

"DO NOT GO TO HIM." Explaining her adamant advice, she adds, "All boyz like a chase. Let Romeo come to u."

Thirty-five

"Lorenzo!"

Enzo's mother calls to the back room of their café. My heart is thudding. Not just from the climb, either. A week has passed since we held hands across the Bridge of the Towers. A *week*! How long does Jackie expect me to lie on my bed listening to stupid birds? The summer is frittering away!

"Ayley!"

Enzo emerges through the swinging door all smiles. He kisses both cheeks and asks, "How are you?"

How am I? I nearly screech. I'm a desperate American girl who has fallen for an Italian boy who refuses to chase her no matter how hard-to-get she pretends to be.

"Fine," I say. "You?"

"Bene," he replies, which I think means *fine*, which is not what I want to hear. I'd been hoping he had a Vespa accident. Not a bad one. Just enough to put him in the hospital for a week. For observation only. Away from friends and family and anyone who could have gotten a message to me.

Now that I'm standing here, in a low-cut T-shirt (Jackie's suggestion) and peach-colored blush to soften my pale cheeks (yeah, Jackie again), I feel like an idiot. Customers are at the tables, he's busy. Pathetically, I'd only thought this through to the moment when Enzo's mother gave me directions to the hospital where her son has been crying out my name.

"Gelato?" Enzo asks.

I swallow a moan. Things are worse than I thought. My standing has plummeted from potential sex object to potential customer. Jackie was right. No matter how long it took, I should have waited. Even a dog won't play with a chew toy unless you wiggle it just out of his reach! The moment Enzo saw that I was his, he decided he'd rather wait on me than jump my bones. When will I ever learn? Why does everyone else know how to be a girlfriend, while I only know how to be a friend?

Frantic to save my peach-colored face, I search my mind for some reason why I'm here. Other than flinging myself at Enzo.

"The lake," I blurt out. "Want to come with me tomorrow?"

"Lake Trasimeno?"

"*Sì.*"

Enzo's face lights up. He says something to his mother in Italian, then turns to me and nods his head happily.

"Good," I say. "Do you happen to know how to get there, and can you drive?"

A *lake*? What am I thinking? Didn't I learn my lesson at the beach with Drew? Not only am I allergic to bathing suits, my pasty-white skin will scorch under the Umbrian sun. As it is, I've already gone through a whole tube of sunscreen this summer. Not that it's stopped the frecklepalooza on my face. Do they have cabanas at a lake? An overturned boat? Enough sand to bury myself?

"We take my Vespa," Enzo offers graciously.

"I'll make lunch," I say. Then, scrambling to follow Jackie's advice, I toss my hair seductively, swivel on my heels, and head back down the hill.

"Catch me if you can," I mumble under my breath, trying to sound sexy. Better late than never. Right?

All the way down, I beat myself up for suggesting such a stupid location. You don't grow up near the *Baywatch* beach and watch every episode of *Survivor* without realizing that natural bodies of water require baring unnatural amounts of skin. Though I am feeling better about my curves, less than half a yard of fabric stretched over my boobs and butt could easily run my progress off the road. I didn't even bring a bathing suit with me to Italy. Why suffer

185

mortification in *two* countries?

"*A domani!*" Enzo shouts after me.

See you tomorrow.

I swallow hard. How much of me did he expect to see?

Thirty-Six

The back road to Lake Trasimeno winds around green fields that are littered with yellow flowers. I'm wearing long shorts and a T-shirt. A wide-brimmed hat is squished into my backpack along with our lunch. The Vespa bumps along, sending up plumes of dust around our ankles. Occasionally, Enzo turns onto a paved street and we pass stone farmhouses that look like pink sandcastles.

It's another perfect day. Except for the dread growing in my gut like a giant gnocchi. What am I going to say when Enzo strips down to his bathing suit, and I merely remove my flip-flops? He won't expect me to swim in my bra and underpants, will he? He's not wearing one of those skimpy Speedos, is he?

Finally, I decide to deal with it while we're still on the road. Before the gnocchi expands and I hurl.

"I can't swim," I say loudly into the helmet covering Enzo's ear. It's not true, of course, but my stressed-out brain can't think of a less embarrassing way to explain why he'll be taking off his clothes and I won't.

Enzo shrugs and yells back, "I can't dance."

We both laugh.

Wrapped around his beautiful back, feeling the ripple of his ribs beneath his shirt, smelling the watermelon scent of the freshly washed hair curling out from the bottom of his helmet, I smile. Yeah, this *is* love.

After an hour, a few minutes, half a day—who can tell in Italian time?—we climb higher up a mountain. The trees get greener and the air gets cooler. Finally, we ride through a town called Borghetto and there it is. The gorgeous lake glistens in the distance. It's far below us. Tiny islands float in the middle like bunches of broccoli spears. Two small fishing boats are anchored offshore. The water is gray-blue, the shoreline seems to be rimmed with trees. This high up the hill, I can't see any sand at all.

Enzo pulls the Vespa over and cuts the engine.

"Why are we stopping?" I ask.

"We arrive," he says.

Confused, I hop off as Enzo rolls the Vespa into a small clearing on the edge of the hill. He stores both our helmets there, too, and takes my hand. Together, we snake down a narrow dirt path. It's silent and scenic. I inhale the vanilla honey scent of flowers and sawed-wood smell of damp earth. The farther we move down the hill, the higher the grass gets. By the time Enzo stops, we're alone on the side of a hill, near a knotty old olive tree, hidden from everyone. Lake Trasimeno stretches out for miles far below.

"My favorite spot in all of Italy," Enzo says softly. "I happy to share it with you."

Enzo flattens the tall grass in a circle and we sit in our own private terrace with a view.

Suddenly, my heart is pumping so hard I hear it in my ears.

"Hungry?" Enzo asks.

Yeah, like I can eat.

"Sure," I say, my voice like a bird call.

Attempting to relax, I slip my flip-flops off and run my toes through flattened soft grass. One by one, I remove the wrapped pieces of our lunch. A chunk of Parmesan cheese, two ripe peaches, flatbread with prosciutto. Everything I hope he likes. Enzo takes out a bottle of water and opens it, giving me the first sip. Amazingly, the water is still chilled. I let my eyes fall closed as I feel the cool water flow down my throat, my esophagus, my stomach. When I open them, Enzo is so close to me I can feel the heat from his body.

"Mia Americana," he says, almost in a whisper.

My heart stops. A trickle of water escapes my mouth and rolls slowly down my chin. Enzo leans in and licks it. Every nerve ending in my body goes berserk. My senses are all on alert. I feel like I can see through walls, hear through mountains. With a sweep of his arm, Enzo pushes our lunch aside and lowers me flat on the grass. Gently, he kisses my chin, my cheek, my eyelashes. When he pulls back, I gaze into eyes as deep and blue as Lake Trasimeno.

"*Bella faccia,*" he murmurs.

I melt into the grass beneath me. When Enzo says I have a pretty face, I feel *beautiful.*

My hand reaches up to touch his face, his hair. Then I pull Enzo to my lips. This kiss is going to count, I say to myself, remembering the slumber party kiss that didn't. I've never felt more awake. With a flicker of my tongue, I separate his lips. I invite him in. We explore my mouth together. His kiss is so full of passion, both our body temperatures spike. I can feel Enzo's heat passing into my chest.

Suddenly, he pulls back and says, "I can't look at you without knowing you will soon leave me."

"Close your eyes," I reply. And I kiss him again. The gap between his two front teeth fills my heart with longing.

With the sun above our heads, the lake down the hill, the smell of prosciutto and Parmesan wafting up from the lunch that's now scattered around our private spot, I feel like my whole life has led to this one moment. Enzo's hands reach under my shirt; my hands reach under his. His skin is as warm and smooth as beach sand. Amazingly, I don't feel self-conscious. I'm not sucking in my gut or obsessing about my butt. Everything feels absolutely right.

"I've never done this before," I whisper, knowing where we're headed.

"Me, either," he says.

His heart is thumping as hard as mine.

"I'm scared," I admit.

"Me, too. We be scared together, no?"

I kiss him again. He presses our hearts together.

"Do you have a condom?" I ask.

"Condom?"

"Protection."

"No," he says. "You?"

"No."

We both groan.

"I be careful," he says, running his fingers gently down my stomach.

"I want to," I say. "But no. Not without protection."

Enzo groans again, falls back on the grass, and mutters words in Italian. By his pained expression, I sense it's something like, "Why me?!"

Before things rev up again and risk going beyond the point of no return, I sit up and say, "I have an idea."

Enzo looks up from the grass.

"Tonight," I say, "meet me at the gate."

He grins and I fall into those blue eyes again.

"Tonight," he says. "I bring condom."

Thirty-Seven

I can't believe I'm doing this. What am I doing!? My brain is firing off a gazillion thoughts at once. Sneaking Enzo up to my room? Should I tell Patrice? What if she says no? Of course she'll say no! My parents didn't send their daughter to Italy so she could lose her virginity! And yet, what could be more perfect? Enzo makes me feel beautiful. Normal. My body is curvy, not fat. My "pretty face" is a compliment instead of a veiled insult. I'm in love. He seems to be, too. Isn't this exactly how your first time—how every time—should be?

Up in my room, back from the lake, I get everything ready. I change my sheets, shower, sweep the stone floor. At dinner, I chat about the beautiful lake and eat lightly. No garlic!

"Is Enzo your boyfriend?" Gianna asks.

"No," I say.

Patrice says, "I like him. He helps his mother."

I say, "I like him, too."

After dinner and the dishes, I tell the De Lucas I'm tired and I'll see them in the morning. Then, I go up to my room and watch Assisi change color in the fading light. By the time it's dark, my brain has fried itself into a peaceful hum. I'm not as nervous as I thought I'd be. I'm excited. Ready.

The crunch of my sandals on the driveway makes me cringe. I tiptoe to the gate. Enzo is already there.

"I afraid you change your mind," he says.

I smile. "No way."

Thankfully, the gate opens silently. Enzo steps through and takes my face in his hands. He kisses me hard, whispers Italian words in my ear.

I say, *"Sì, sì,"* though I have no idea what he says.

Holding his hand, I lead him back up the path to my tower. He gasps at the sight of the De Lucas' stunning house. His hand goes over his heart when I show him La Torre. Slowly, we climb the outdoor spiral staircase. Our shoes tap the metal steps. At the top, in the light of the moon, Enzo kisses me again.

"I can't help it," he says. And I can't stop smiling.

Inside, I put a chair against the door. Just in case. There isn't a lock. I'd hate to have Gianna decide she wants a late-night chat with her American "sister." Before I can turn back around, Enzo steps up behind me. He presses his body against mine, and kisses the back of my neck. I fall into him, *feel* him touching me.

"*Te adoro,*" he says softly.

The hawk outside my window cries out. Enzo stops.

"Listen," he says. The hawk wails again. A loud shrill cry. "Hear the loneliness? He call for his mate."

We stand quietly for a moment, listening, until something magical happens. For the first time, I hear another hawk answer back. It's still a sharp cry, but it's clearly different.

Enzo turns me around and says, "They find each other at last."

My whole body melts into Enzo's deep kiss. He lifts my shirt over my head and I unbutton his. My shirt gets caught on my nose, his buttons are impossibly tiny. We're both shaking. Finally, both bare-chested, I kiss his smooth brown chest. He bends over to kiss my back. Chills run through my whole body.

"Ayley," he whispers.

"Entzo," I whisper back.

In a clumsy dance of love, we end up naked, in each other's arms on top of my bed. Enzo fumbles with the condom; I try to calm my thudding heart. Frantically, I think back to Health class. Did I ever learn exactly what I'm supposed to *do*? Not that I can move. Enzo plants another kiss on my lips. Instantly, I melt into his warm body and feel myself letting go. Condom in place, we both give ourselves to the other for the very first time. It's awkward, sensual, embarrassing, painful for a second, and utterly *right*. Enzo is the boy I've waited for all my life.

Thirty-Eight

"You look different," Patrice says, eyeing me the next morning at breakfast.

Enzo left after midnight. He knew his mother would worry if he stayed out longer. Through my open window, I heard the faint putter of his Vespa on the road. For a long time, I stared at the beautiful illuminated hill of Assisi, imagining his ascent. Is he past the piazza yet? Climbing the stairs yet? Where does he park the Vespa? All the way up that enormous staircase?

"I am different," I say, meeting Patrice's gaze. "Italy has finally seeped into my soul."

She cups my chin. "If Italy gets in anywhere else," she says quietly, "make sure you're careful."

I nod. Once again, I wonder how this totally cool

woman could ever be friends with my mother.

Enzo has to work today, so I set out early to climb the hill and help him. His mother kisses my cheeks when she sees me. Enzo tells her to take the day off. "*Ayley* is *ere* to *elp* me," he says, dropping all the "h"s.

"*Grazie mille,*" she says to me, tearing up. At that moment I realize how hard it's been for her. Raising two boys all alone. Running a business with so few days off.

"*Prego,*" I reply, glad to help out.

Enzo and I watch his mother make her way down the staircase into town. A few moments later, a large group of tourists make their way up. Gasping the way I did my first journey to the café, they stagger to the tables. I ask the obvious question: Gelato?

We're busy all day. It's fun. Enzo nuzzles my neck when no one is watching. I chat with the Americans and Brits; he chats with the Italians and Spanish. Together we try our best to communicate with the French. It's a United Nations in the café. Must be tourist season, I chuckle to myself. By the end of the day, Enzo and I are both tired. Exhilarated, but exhausted.

"We have dinner up here in Assisi," he suggests.

"Cool," I say, calling Patrice to tell her I won't be home until after dark.

"Do I need to worry?" she asks me.

"No," I reply. And I mean it. I've never felt more safe in my life.

||||||||||||||||||

197

As soon as the sun goes down, Enzo's mother returns. We've already washed the tables and chairs outside, swept the floor inside, and cleaned all the counters. She's thrilled to see how well everything went, and insists we enjoy an evening in town. I brush my hair, reapply gloss, and hold Enzo's hand as we walk into town. Halfway down the stairs, beneath the only light that illuminates the staircase at night, he wraps both arms around me and kisses me hard.

"I waited to do this all day," he says.

We laugh. Kiss once more. Then walk the rest of the way down the stairs to spend the evening on a typical Italian date.

"Enzo!"

"Stefano!"

"Florencia!"

"Cesare!"

"Lucia!"

It doesn't take long for Enzo to run into a bunch of friends. He introduces me and before I know it, we're all sitting in a trattoria, under the moonlight, eating pasta and drinking red wine.

Though everybody speaks English to be polite to me, I barely understand what they're saying. It's all politics and world events. Totally unlike a group of friends in California. I can't imagine anyone *thinking* about global issues, much less talking intelligently about them. Unless, of course, it's how global warming is making all the SUV hogs feel guilty.

"What do you think about China?" Cesare asks me.

My heart lurches. "I prefer it to paper plates," I say.

There's silence for a moment, then everyone laughs.

"Funny *Americana*," says Cesare. I laugh, too. I like the sound of that. Of me being *me*.

Dinner lasts for hours. The waiter doesn't seem to care that we're just sitting there. One of the girls smokes a cigarette and nobody freaks out. There's an ease to the group that comes with kids who've known one another their whole lives. And they totally accept me. I don't feel like the "fat girl." I'm just me. Hayley. *Ayley.* The curvy girl with the pretty face.

Plus, the pasta was to die for.

Thirty-Nine

Enzo and I see each other almost every day—and many nights—for the rest of the summer. We fall easily into the gentle rhythm of Italy.

"I'll wait for you at the fountain," Enzo says, whenever he knows he'll have time off.

I climb the stairs to help out at the café whenever he doesn't.

In the late afternoon, we take long walks down the back hill of Assisi, ride bikes to the next village, take the Vespa into the next town.

"Do you know where I can buy a Francesco Totti soccer jersey for my brother?" I ask Enzo.

He points. "There, there, there. Totti is hero. You

can buy everywhere!"

I buy a jersey for my brother, a hand-painted platter for my mother, and a great bottle of wine for my dad. As I pay for them, I see the sadness in Enzo's eyes and feel the heaviness in my heart. Nobody buys souvenirs unless they're getting ready to leave.

In the late afternoon over espresso, in the evening over supper, or at night after we secretly make love, Enzo and I get to know each other in that condensed way you do when you know time is running out.

"Do you see yourself running the café in the future?" I ask one day.

"I don't see the future," Enzo replies. "I see this moment."

"If you could have one wish, what would it be?" I ask another day.

"To stop time," he says.

"If you could live anywhere in the world, where would you live?"

"Right here," Enzo replies. "In your arms."

He's nothing like any boy I've ever met. It may be Italy, or it may be Enzo, but I'm agog at his openness. When I asked why he didn't try to find me the day after we first met, he said, "I wait to make sure you want me, too." When I nervously asked if my body was okay, he answered, "No. It is *perfect* because it is the only house of you."

How do you leave a guy like that? How do you get on a

plane and fly back to a city where *no one* feels like they have a perfect house of you?

Neither one of us talks about my departure. But as the days pass, Enzo's kisses grow more intense. My hand squeezes his at midnight, unable to bear letting it, or him, go.

"Memorize every moment," I say to myself. And I do.

"Benvenuto!" Gino says to Enzo when he arrives one morning while we're all eating breakfast. *"Che cosa preferisce?"*

"I eat already, *grazie*," he says. "But I love a coffee."

"I get a cup," Gianna says, rising and running into the house.

Enzo sits and chats with Gino in Italian. Patrice smiles at me and kisses the top of Taddeo's head. I finish my biscotti and bowl of fresh strawberries. It all feels so natural, my heart aches. The De Lucas welcomed Enzo into their family as easily as his mother welcomed me. There was no third degree like there would be at my parents' table. No one cared if Enzo was going to college or getting good grades or aware that there are seventeen fat grams in a patty of beef.

"I want to take Ayley to the lake today," Enzo says to Patrice. "Okay to have her all day?"

"Can Romy and I go?" Gianna squeals, returning from the kitchen with a cup for Enzo's coffee.

"No," Patrice says. "Our family will go another time."

Turning to Enzo, Patrice says, "Take care of our girl." Then she adds, "Though I know she can take care of herself."

It's early September. The sun is more gold than yellow, the air tickles my cheeks. I'm going home soon. It's too sad to think about, so I don't. I refuse to let anything ruin our last day at the lake.

On the winding back roads to Lake Trasimeno, I wrap my arms tightly around Enzo's waist. I reach under his shirt and feel the warmth of his skin. With each inhalation, I try to memorize his smell. I want to take his shirt home with me, like a puppy who sleeps with his master's clothes, so I won't forget him. But how could I? How do you forget the boy who makes you finally like yourself?

We park the Vespa at the top of the hill and make our way down to "our" spot—the place where we first kissed. Silently, Enzo flattens the grass. He takes my hand and gently pulls me to the ground next to him. Together, in the shadow of the olive tree, overlooking the glimmering lake, we give ourselves to each other one last time.

"*Ti amo*," Enzo whispers. I inhale sharply. I know that word from Latin class.

Amare. Amo. Amas. Amat.

To love. I love. You love. He loves.

"*Ti amo, anche,*" I say.

I love you, too.

Forty

"I was, like, get *out*. He was, like, come *on.*"

"Send the limo to the *front.* I'm not paying you so I can walk."

"Put the nanny on the phone."

Los Angeles after Assisi feels like a fire hose blast of cold water. I was numb on the plane. Now, the harsh glare of the airport wakes me up.

"Have my agent call his agent and we'll do lunch."

Everyone has a cell pressed to their heads. The snippets of conversation feel like pinpricks in my ear.

"He's the *nose* guy. Doctor *Tommy* is the boob guy."

"Hayley!"

My mother rushes to greet me in the arrivals area of LAX.

"You've lost weight!" she squeals. "Our plan worked! I'm going to catch the next plane to Italy!"

"Welcome home, honey," Dad says, kissing my forehead.

"Did you remember my Totti shirt?" asks Quinn, right behind him.

"You'll need new clothes for your new body," Mom chirps. "When can we hit the mall together? Just us girls!"

My family shoots questions at me so quickly I barely have a chance to answer. But, by the time we're sitting in traffic on the Santa Monica Freeway, breathing the exhaust from bumper-to-bumper gas-guzzlers, it's beginning to sink in that I'm actually home.

I'm here.

He's there.

A country and an ocean are between us.

"As a treat for your first night back," Mom says, "we're all going out for veggie pizza at Domino's!"

My mind is swirling. Is it possible I kissed Enzo good-bye *last night*? Was I in Rome this morning?

Enzo didn't come to the airport with the De Lucas and me.

"I want to remember you here," he said, "in Assisi."

That's how I wanted to remember me, too. In my tower

overlooking the beautiful mountain. My head resting on Enzo's warm chest.

We barely said anything on our last night together. Promises seemed hollow, whispers of love hurt too much. So we let our bodies speak. By the time the sun came up, he was gone. A single rose petal from Patrice's garden lay on his pillow. I held it in my hand, inhaled its scent, and burst into tears. Is this all that's left of the boy I love? Will I ever see Enzo again?

"For you," Taddeo had said at the airport, handing me the frog he so lovingly cared for all summer.

My eyes instantly flooded with tears. I took the frog in my hands, felt its racing heartbeat. Then I held the tiny frog up to my ear.

"Oh, no," I'd said. "He only speaks Italian!"

The De Lucas laughed. Gently passing the frog back to Taddeo, I told him, "I think he wants to stay here. This is his home."

Taddeo happily tucked the frog back in his pocket. Before we could say anything else, the loudspeaker announced my flight. It was time to say good-bye.

"Ayley."

Patrice and Gino hugged me together.

"You are *famiglia* now," Gino said. My summer in Italy let me know how special that statement really was.

"*Grazie mille,*" I said, hugging them both even tighter.

Behind us, Gianna looked like an orphan. She stood alone, crying. I went to her, gave her a tissue, and asked, "Will you take care of my purples in the garden?"

She sniffed, nodded.

"Will you come and visit me someday?"

Gianna shrugged slightly. I added, "We'll look for Britney's house together."

In spite of herself, Gianna grinned. "Can Romy come, too?"

"I wouldn't have it any other way."

With kisses all around, and a heart ready to burst, my amazing summer came to an end. Now, I'm here. On the other side of the world. Eating a slice of Domino's pizza. Trying to explain to my family—my *real* family—how ten weeks in another country can change a person for life.

"How does Patrice look?" Mom asks.

"Beautiful," I answer. "Centered and happy."

"Has she kept her figure?"

I remember the photos of Patrice and my mom on the beach. "She's traded it in for a more practical model," I reply.

Mom's eyebrows scrunch up. "How can anyone maintain her weight with all that pasta?" she asks, picking a broccoli spear off her pizza and nibbling at it. Dad and Quinn fight over the last Cheesy Breadstick.

"We walk around a lot," I say.

"What do you mean, *we*?" Mom scoffs.

My hand flies up to my mouth. I laugh nervously and say, "Oops." Then, the same feeling of homesickness I felt in Italy washes over me. My heart aches for the purples in the garden, the red towels in the bathroom, the orange glow of Assisi. Most of all, I long for the milk-chocolate brown of that soft spot under Enzo's chin that I love to kiss.

"Are you okay?" Mom says.

"Who's up for ice cream?" Dad asks, hopeful.

Quinn squeals, "Me! Me!" as I nod at my mother. It's a lie, of course. I'm not okay. Not yet. But, for the first time ever, I'm beginning to understand exactly how I feel, who I really am. I'm not the fat girl with the untanned skin who hates the sun and the sand. I'm *Hayley*—sad sometimes, happy most of the time, hungry on occasion, full of determination, curvy, smart, funny, and (finally!) able to feel—really *feel*—honest, genuine, deep, authentic, totally true love.

I'm me—the girl with the pretty face.

Forty-One

"Hayley!" Jackie hugs me so hard I feel like a tube of tooth-paste.

The day after I arrive home, we meet on a bench by the beach. She's crying and I'm gasping and we both can't wait to relive our summers through the eyes of our BFFs.

"You look awesome!" she says.

"You do, too," I say, hugging her back.

"It's true, then," she says.

"What?"

"Losing your V totally changes your bod!"

I laugh. "Banning fast food and chugging my butt up a humongous hill every day helped, too."

Jackie sniffs hard. "This was the longest summer of my life."

"The shortest summer of mine," I say.

"Have you heard from him?" she asks, drying her eyes.

"Yes," I say, "but he doesn't have a computer! I have to wait for him to go to the Internet café in town! It's the middle of the night!"

"Hello! Just like I had to do all summer!"

We laugh. Hug each other again.

"I wish Drew could see you now," Jackie says. "His jaw would drop."

Drew. The sound of Drew Wyler's name sends an unfamiliar sensation through my body: *Nothing.* My crush on Drew is as far away as Lake Trasimeno. The only thing I feel right now is curiosity.

"What's up with him?" I ask. "And you?"

Jackie sighs. "Drew got busted out of Pacific High."

"No!"

"Yes. Somehow the school found out and he's spending his senior year in *Inglewood.*"

"Oh, no!"

"Oh, yes."

"Are you bummed beyond belief?" I ask my best friend.

"Not really," she says. "We never had a serious thing. I'm still saving my V for Wenty. Or Worthy. Whatever I'm going to call him. If only I could get him to call me."

We laugh again. Suddenly, I realize how much I missed Jackie. Not until this very moment did I allow myself to feel it. She's part of my life, just as Enzo is now part of my heart.

"Promise me you'll never leave me again," Jackie says.

"Come with me next time," I say.

"Next time?"

"Honestly, Jackie, except for you, I'd do anything to go back."

"Can't you carry Italy with you in *here*?" She points to my heart.

"That's what Enzo says," I say. And I miss him all over again.

Forty-Two

Long-distance relationships suck. Especially if the distance is five thousand miles. And the relationship is your first ever, and the sex was truly making *love*, and you're sure you'll die if you can't kiss him in the next twenty-four hours.

"Bella faccia," Enzo IMs me.

I've come to love those two words: Pretty face. I can still hear his voice, feel the tickle of his breath on my ear.

"I'm here," I write. It's one in the morning. Where else would I be?

"Too much miles between us."

"Sì."

"When you come back?"

I sigh. School starts next week. Senior year. SATs.

College apps. Essays on the color red. Mom keeps bugging me to go to the Promenade with her.

"They're having a sale at Abercrombie and Fitch!" she says, thrilled that they'll now have my size. Yesterday was the first day I stepped on my talking scale. For the first time in forever, I liked what I heard. I missed my goal of losing thirty pounds by eating less than a thousand calories a day. Instead, I gained my *soul* by slowing down, tasting every bite, loving every flavor, and exercising more than a short walk to my car.

I'm still round, but I'm no longer fat. I'm in my own perfect house of me.

"I don't know," I write to Enzo. "When can you come here?"

Across the ocean, I hear his sigh. It took Enzo two years to save for his Vespa. His mother doesn't have much money, either.

"Someday," Enzo types.

"Yeah," I reply. "Someday."

I can still see Assisi glowing in its golden light. When I shut my eyes, I smell the flowers, hear the hawk cry for its mate. I fall into the gap between Enzo's front teeth.

"Until I see you, Hayley," Enzo types, "hold me in your heart."

His gentle voice is in my ears. "Ayley, *old* me in your *eart.*"

"You're already there," I write.

"Brava," he writes back. "We are together forever now."